THE Quiet Triumph OF Rachel Farrowsworth

ALISON SWEENEY

First published in Australia by Aurora House
www.aurorahouse.com.au

This edition published 2022
Copyright © Alison Sweeney 2022

Cover design: Donika Mishineva | www.artofdonika.com
Typesetting and e-book design: Amit Dey

ISBN number: 978-1-922697-85-1 (Paperback)

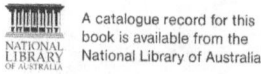
A catalogue record for this
book is available from the
National Library of Australia

Distributed by: Ingram Content: www.ingramcontent.com
Australia: phone +613 9765 4800 |
email lsiaustralia@ingramcontent.com
Milton Keynes UK: phone +44 (0)845 121 4567 |
email enquiries@ingramcontent.com
La Vergne, TN USA: phone +1 800 509 4156 |
email inquiry@lightningsource.com

About the Author

After more than twenty years in Human Resources Alison decided she preferred words to people and went on to fulfil a career in Communications.

Born in Calcutta to a Scottish mother and an Anglo-Indian father she describes herself as being pale with a liking for a curry.

She lives in Sydney and is married to a Kiwi.

You can connect with Alison on Twitter https://twitter.com/Blend_Of_Stuff or on Facebook at https://www.facebook.com/BlendOfStuff.

Visit Alison's blog https://theinstantcoffee.com/

This is her first novel.

Chapter One

'Older Australians should stay in the labour market and work until they're seventy,' the Federal Treasurer droned.

Rachel scowled and looked up from inspecting her one good 'interview' blouse.

The way I'm going, I'll still be looking for a job when I'm seventy.

Suddenly noticing the time and, hoping no one would spot the slightly frayed collar if she tucked it neatly under her jacket, she turned off the radio. The flat fell silent once more, save for the thundering traffic noise (a disadvantage of only being able to afford to rent on a busy road).

Rachel looked in the mirror — not quite a full length and with a crack down the middle — and was immediately disheartened. Even if the mirror had been spotlessly clean in a private dressing room at David Jones, she thought wryly, it wouldn't have made much of a difference.

Brown was the colour of the suit. It wasn't a warm chocolaty brown, either, but a dismal colour that looked like a stained carpet in an old country RSL. It was also baggy on her, which didn't help matters. Her blouse was cream with a high neckline. She had been overjoyed when she discovered it in an op shop. It complemented her colouring, and (frayed collar aside) she was grateful for that – if ever she needed a lift, today was the day.

She had an interview! A real face-to-face interview. Rachel checked her bag (brown) for her meagre possessions. Wallet, her precious Opal card, her old phone (cracked), tissues, face mask, keys, and the piece of paper with the details of the interview she'd carefully written out.

Confident she had everything, she lifted her shoulder bag only for it to immediately crash to the floor leaving her helplessly holding a broken strap. Sweating and holding back tears, she shoved everything back into the bag, clutching it to her chest as she locked the door. The broken bag strap felt like a bad omen, and as she walked briskly to the station, she tried to calm her nerves.

It was only a five-minute walk to the station and after sending a prayer of thanks (misguided given she had no time for religion) to Sydney Trains that there were no delays, she boarded the 8.20 am to Town Hall.

It was a tight squash. Even though social distancing was encouraged in the wake of COVID-19, most early morning train commuters prioritised the comfort of a seat rather than safeguarding themselves against a deadly virus. Rachel donned her mask and found herself sandwiched between a large man playing a game on his computer and a young girl putting on her make-up. Rachel sat transfixed as all manner of make-up was produced from her cavernous bag — foundation, mascara, blusher, lip products. Rachel looked down at her cracked hands and wondered how the girl — with her sleek black hair, dark sculpted eyebrows, expertly applied ruby red lips, and a hint of expensive perfume — would react if Rachel told her she couldn't afford to buy any make-up and only owned one precious lipstick (now worn down to a stub) which she kept for days like today.

I don't belong here.

As was always the case, she was early. She had purposely got an early train — there was no way she could have survived the stress of running late — and now she had thirty minutes to kill. She was too nervous to sit, her hands were already sweating and despite the cool March morning, she felt beads of moisture on her forehead. Great, she thought, what a winning combination — a hot flush and nervous sweating! Rachel looked enviously at the people casually buying their morning coffee and toast. She couldn't afford a coffee, and it seemed like hours since she'd hurriedly eaten a banana for her breakfast.

Rachel suddenly felt her heart racing; negative thoughts pulsated through her mind. She looked at her shaking hands and tried a technique she'd been taught years ago. *Deep breath. Slow deep breath. In. Out. In. Out. That's it, that's better. Now, acknowledge three things I can hear. Buses. I hear buses. High heels. A group of women are walking past, and I can hear the click of their heels. Breath. In. Out. A busker. I can hear a guitar being played.* Rachel's heart rate settled. She opened her eyes. She felt better. She was ready.

Arriving at the recruitment agency at precisely 9.45 am, she was instantly intimidated by the sleek and sophisticated reception area, with its glass tables, white walls, and soft lighting.

'Good morning, my name is Rachel Farrowsworth, and I have an interview with Tiffany Reece at 10 am.' She had practiced in front of the mirror, and her voice did not let her down, despite her nerves.

'Yes, Rachel, now I'll just get you to take a seat and complete this,' said the receptionist, barely glancing at her as she turned back to laugh with her colleague at something they were looking at on their phones.

Rachel sat down, placing her bag at her feet. Name, address. *Why do I have to do all of this again, as I gave them my information when I applied?*

What made you apply for this position? *Because I'm out of work and I need to eat and pay bills.* What a silly question, thought Rachel. But no matter, she'd prepared for this. She consulted her notes and wrote: *The position sounds rewarding and a good fit for my skills and experience. I believe I'd be an asset to the company.* Rachel again breathed deeply to calm herself as she completed the form.

Behind the vast reception area, in an open-plan office that hummed under a potent aroma of coffee and perfume, Tiffany Reece yawned as she glanced at the application in front of her. The job she was trying to fill was for an Administrative Assistant for a hair product company. Answering phones, paperwork, data entry, sales orders.

Tiffany sighed as she looked enviously at some of her colleagues, working with start-ups and technology companies. She plastered on a smile, trying to look enthusiastic as she walked briskly in her towering stilettos to reception.

'Hi Rachel, I'm Tiffany. Would you like to come through?'

Suddenly there was a thud. Rachel had bent down to lift her bag and had forgotten about the broken strap. The splattered contents were there for all to see on the glossy white floor. Tiffany, immaculate in a tight black pencil skirt and pale blue silk blouse, clucked her tongue with a disapproving 'tsk, tsk', before bending down to pick up Rachel's one good lipstick and slowly handing it back to her.

Rachel was not surprised to receive the oh-so-standard rejection email in her inbox four days later, given it was clear Tiffany lost interest in her five minutes after meeting her.

'So, you were a hairdresser, back in um?' Tiffany had seemed more interested in her perfectly manicured nails than in Rachel's resume.

'In the 1980s,' said Rachel.

'And since then?'

'I've gained a lot of administrative experience, I've worked in call centres, so I'm good with customers,' mumbled Rachel, put off by the woman's obvious disinterest in her.

'So, Hair'N'Now, as you know, make a range of very popular hair products, and they're growing. They promote a fun work environment. How would you contribute to that?' asked Tiffany.

'Fun?'

'Yes,' said Tiffany impatiently.

'Well, I like to laugh. Um, is that what you mean?' said Rachel.

Rachel felt Tiffany's disapproving gaze on her, taking in the brownness, the greying hair, the bitten nails, the beads of sweat on her unmade-up face.

It's not easy looking for a job when you're fifty-six and a woman.

The weather on Tuesday morning mirrored her attitude: dreary and overcast. Rachel hung up the tea towel after rinsing her coffee cup and cereal bowl, before looking at the list she had jotted down earlier.

If you asked her what the most important thing in her life was, she'd probably say that "writing lists" was towards the top of the, well, list.

- Library – email, jobs
- Check bank account
- Ring nursing home
- Buy tea
- Ring Rosie!
- Go to op shop.

Rachel sighed and looked around her. The unit was in a large block in South West Sydney. There was, of course, no balcony and on a day like today there was no sun piercing through the threadbare curtains. The only sounds were the never-ending throb of traffic noise and the dripping of the tap in the basin where her underwear lay soaking.

Suddenly 'ring Rosie' was at the top of her list.

Rachel and Rosie had met on their first day of high school. Somehow, they had ended up sitting together and their new teacher made a cheesy remark about how cute their names sounded combined. Rachel had given Rosie a hesitant look, expecting rejection. Rosie, on the other hand, answered with a big grin and an exaggerated eye roll. They'd been best friends ever since.

'I didn't get that job,' she said when Rosie answered.

'Their loss,' said Rosie, just as she always did.

Rachel nibbled at her nails as she pictured Rosie. She was probably in her kitchen, where she spent most of her time, all manner of paraphernalia strewn across the large kitchen island benchtop; a cup of coffee on the go, her mop of untamed flame-red hair pulled back with an elastic band. Rachel thought of her own thin straight brown hair, just one of their many differences.

They were devoted to one another. Rachel was godmother to Rosie's two children. Rosie relied on Rachel's thoughtful, calm demeanour, whereas Rachel needed the push and straight-talking her boisterous friend provided.

Rosie believed that every 'win', no matter how minor or insignificant, should be celebrated, something she picked up in one of the many self-help books she consumed (much to the chagrin of her long-suffering husband). Rachel couldn't function without her. She was the one she always turned to with good or bad news, and even though she lived in Melbourne, they were never out of touch.

Rachel recounted what the recruiter had said about contributing to fun in the workplace.

Rosie snorted down the phone, 'What do they want you to do? A stand-up routine while you're typing?'

Rosie cheered her up as she often did. But Rachel stopped laughing and became serious when Rosie proposed the next time she was asked such a silly question, she should tell them she was a well-known pole dancer on the side and casually enquire whether that would be enough 'fun'?

'What am I going to do, Rosie? I need to get a job, and I need it now.'

'I'm sure we could—'

'No.'

Rosie and her husband Bruce had lent Rachel money when things were bad (much worse than they were now). She knew that things weren't exactly going well for them (Bruce had also lost his sales position owing to COVID-19); and she had her pride.

'You know how much I appreciate what you've done for me, but...,' her voice trailed off.

'I get it,' said Rosie.

That night she couldn't sleep. She stared at the peeling paint on the ceiling, tracing the shapes in the darkness. Like the others who had been let go, Rachel was surprised when she was made redundant from her job at a large office supply company after seven years, but she assumed she'd have no trouble finding another job. That was almost three years ago. She reflected on how naive she had been. She picked up occasional casual work, but she knew she had to work full-time to make ends meet.

This isn't living.

Rachel tightened the thin blanket around her shoulders. She appreciated the government help and assistance, but it was always a juggling act — food, bills, rent, phone, medicine. Sometimes she had nothing for food, which was why she was so grateful for charities like Anglicare and the Salvation Army.

Last week, on the phone to Rosie, she had railed against the system.

'I know I have to apply for a certain number of jobs each month, and I do that! I go to all my appointments with my Jobactive provider, I go to EVERY job interview I'm offered.' Rachel was close to tears, but Rosie let her vent.

'It makes me so angry, there are so few full-time jobs and so many casual jobs!'

'I know,' soothed Rosie. 'You'd think the Government would want people getting into full-time work, so they don't have to keep subsidising.'

Rachel didn't seem to hear her. 'People don't seem interested in my years of experience. They just seem to see I'm over fifty and that's that,' said Rachel angrily.

When things were bad and she couldn't afford to pay rent, she'd been forced to take a room in a pub. She knew it was a luxury in comparison to living on the streets, but the room smelled of stale beer and cigarettes, and it was covered in dirt and grime. Cockroaches would dart across the linoleum floor. A visit to the shared bathroom was an act of bravery. She'd hear drunken voices in the corridor and clumsy hands rattling her door handle on numerous occasions. She would rush out of bed and sit with her back against the door, terrified she was going to be attacked. Or worse.

In contrast, she thought, this flat was a palace, even though anyone who saw it would probably disagree. It was no surprise the rent was low. It was painted a dull brown (more peeling than paint) and had a thin cream carpet that was now an indiscriminate shade of brown, bare in many places. *Perhaps that's why I was drawn to the brown suit,* she thought wryly.

The living room and kitchen were practically one room. The tiny kitchen had a sink, a two-burner camp stove, and a small bar fridge. There was a vinyl couch with a couple of awkwardly positioned springs visible. She'd found two old dining chairs on the street to match the previous tenant's small coffee table. Apart from that, the lounge room was bare. The lights were dull. The bathroom had been painted a garish mauve, and no amount of scrubbing could get rid of the mould on the tiles. The flat was cold in winter and hot in summer. She didn't have a washing machine, so if she couldn't afford to go to the laundromat, everything had to be hand-washed and hung up inside, adding to the general gloom.

It did, however, have a locked door, and the old single bed was surprisingly comfortable.

Her situation was precarious. It followed her around at all hours of the day and night, making her sweat and shake. She'd always been frugal, but she'd never been late on her rent.
She couldn't afford to eat some days, but she always comforted herself that as long as she could pay the rent, she'd be fine.

But what if I can't?

Chapter Two

In the morning, there was a knock on her door. It was Rima from next door; her smiling face always a welcome sight for Rachel.

'Here, you eat, breakfast for you,' said Rima pushing an alfoil wrapped package into her hands.

'Rima, oh I can't take this from you.'

'We have, you eat,' said Rima pushing aside her protests. With that, she smiled again, patted Rachel's hand and disappeared back into what was probably early morning chaos corralling her toddler Amira and baby Jamal.

Rachel went back into her unit. She already knew what was in the package, she'd been on the receiving end of Rima's kindness many times. Yum. Pita bread, a hard-boiled egg, and a homemade yoghurt Rima said was called labneh.

She owed much to the little Syrian family next door during the COVID-19 lockdown. She had spent a lot of time with Rima and her husband Ali; little Amira (boss of the household) called her Auntie Rachel.

Rachel's eyes had been opened when she learnt about the family's plight. They had been living in Aleppo, Syria — Rachel had to look up where it was in an atlas from the library — but their apartment had been bombed during one of the many airstrikes. The family fled to Iraq, where they remained for three years until, in search of a better life, they were finally granted a UN humanitarian visa to come to Australia. And to think, they ended up in the unit next to her, on a busy road in South West Sydney.

Rima was one of the kindest people Rachel had ever met. She had stunning dark eyes and a smile that could melt even the coldest heart. Rima taught her what a hijab was and why she wore one. Ali kept a low profile and a close eye on things. Rima claimed Ali was still haunted by what he witnessed during the war. They both lost their parents, as well as many other family members. Rachel occasionally heard Ali crying out in the middle of the night. Nightmares, Rima lamented. She admired the family's bravery — Ali worked as a security guard but hoped to study to become a teacher; Rima worked as a machinist in a factory, sometimes she was even able to do some sewing at home. It was only a few hours here and there, and the pay was low, but it was something, she'd told Rachel when she finally secured the work.

Energised, Rachel headed for the library. The streets were crowded as usual. She'd never lived in such a culturally diverse area before. As she walked, she heard snatches of different languages; Arabic, Vietnamese, Cantonese. She liked peering into some of the small restaurants and eating houses and while she didn't have the means to eat in any of them (or maybe even the confidence given she'd been brought up on a typically Australian diet of meat and three veg) she liked reading the menus and trying to work out what the different foods were. For the first time she noticed the number of 'For lease' signs; many small businesses sadly impacted by COVID-19 lockdowns.

The library, as always, was a welcoming haven. She used the library's computers because she didn't own a computer or have an internet connection at home. Helen, the friendly front-desk employee who assisted her in creating an email address and showed her how to use the computer and printer, smiled warmly at her.

It was busy at the library. In one of the meeting rooms, an English class was in full swing. Rima often attended classes but from what Rachel could make out seemed to spend most of her time making sure everyone had eaten enough of the food she'd made especially for them. In another corner filled with coloured bean bags and large cushions, a group of pre-schoolers were being read a story. In the central reading area, where the sun was blazing in through a strategically positioned skylight, an elderly man was dozing, a newspaper balanced precariously on his knees. An old woman dressed neatly in head-to-toe navy was engrossed in a romance novel.

Rachel began to feel more hopeful as the computer sprang to life and others around her went about their daily routines.

Ten minutes later, she sat holding her head in her hands, her cheerful mood gone as she counted twenty-three more rejection emails. She sighed heavily as she turned away from the computer, hoping to calm herself before she again started trawling the job sites.

'Looking for work is so dehumanising.' A fellow job seeker at the library had summed it up perfectly last week. The woman, perhaps a bit younger than Rachel, had been using the computer next to her and hadn't hidden her bitterness.

Rachel had agreed. Most of the time, you couldn't even speak with the actual employer because everything was handled through recruitment consultants; and she tried not to be ageist, but there was no escaping the fact she was a woman in her mid-fifties trying to persuade people thirty years younger than her that she was worth hiring.

Not hearing anything after working so hard on an application made her feel insignificant in the most demoralising way. Her application to a local real estate agent looking for a part-time administrative assistant four weeks earlier had gotten no response at all. Last week, she'd walked past their office on her way to the bus stop and, looking inside and seeing the staff laughing together, she felt angry. She wasn't sure whether it was their smugness that irritated her — did they know how lucky they were? — or that they did not even reply.

One of the trainers at a job seeker support service explained many recruiters used computer software that could assess hundreds of resumes by using something called 'keywords' to decide who to interview. While she didn't understand all the detail, what she did understand was that a lot of the time no one read the cover letter and resume that people like herself had sweated over. It all seemed so unfair; sitting in the library applying for jobs, her future determined by a machine rather than a human. It drained her confidence and made her feel even less valued than she already did.

Rachel had had a difficult time at school. Today, it would have been diagnosed as dyslexia. She was labelled a 'slow learner' back then, and while a couple of teachers did their best to help her with the time they had, she always struggled with her reading and writing. Rosie had been her champion, helping her with her homework and defending her from bullies who called her 'stupid'.

Despite using computers and relying on spell-check, it added an extra layer of stress to the already stressful activity of looking for a job, let alone being in a job and trying not to make mistakes.

Rachel wondered (not for the first time) if the people making these decisions truly understood what she was going through.

Rachel reflected she had learnt one new skill: she'd become an expert at deciphering job advertisements.

Entry-level meant don't bother applying if you're over twenty-five. Same with any advert that mentions *fun* or *fast-paced* or *dynamic*.

Innovative was code for 'we only want young people to apply as we don't think anyone over the age of forty can be creative'.

For the umpteenth time she wondered why there were so many ads saying *If you're just starting out, we want to hear from you'* when the same job could be done by someone midway or at the end of their career? Surely it was up to the person applying for the job as to whether they wanted to do the required tasks.

The ability to work at home meant you had to have a modern computer, phone and, ideally, an established home office.

We're unable to provide specific feedback on your application meant we expect to be inundated with applications so don't bother applying and if you do, don't expect us to get back to you.

She was astounded by the stereotyping. There appeared to be an assumption that older workers 'live in the past,' unable or unwilling to learn new skills. Rachel had met a lot of people her age (and older) looking for work, and nothing could be further from the truth.

All she needed was one person to believe in her. She didn't want to think about how many jobs she'd applied for in the previous year, but she guessed it was at least a few hundred.

A few hours later after sending off another twelve applications, Rachel treated herself to a half-hour in the sunny reading area. An old man was engrossed in his Chinese newspaper. A woman wearing a burka (she'd learnt the word from Rima) was reading a book, her solemn dark-eyed daughter at her feet. A young mother was patiently telling her son that he could only borrow three books, not the twenty or so they had accumulated. Rachel picked up one of the women's magazines and sighed with pleasure. She always gave this half-hour to herself, a time to try and forget her situation.

Her phone beeped. Rosie was reading another self-help book, this time one of Oprah's. She braced herself: *Everything happens for a reason, even when we are not wise enough to see it. When there is no struggle, there is no strength.* Hmm.

Turning the page Rachel grinned as she came upon one of those celebrity *A Day in the Life* columns. Who doesn't aspire to start the day with a *Moon Juice Vanilla Mushroom Adaptogenic Protein* smoothie like Gwyneth? Or end the day like Elle *I lie on the bed with my legs up against a wall for at least 10 minutes* Macpherson?

She and Rosie loved them because they were so far removed from their days; they would both be helpless with laughter whenever they read them together and compared them to real life:

- Start the day with a shot of apple cider vinegar to remove toxins (Go to the toilet)
- Get ready for the photoshoot (Brush hair and clean teeth)
- Leisurely scroll through Instagram while sipping a decaf-no-foam-skim-latte-double-shot with a drizzle of caramel (Listen to the radio because I don't have social media)
- Chat with the stylist about clothes (Put on my second-hand clothes)
- Graze on fresh organic almond butter with celery, and one walnut (Have a banana)
- OMG, how good do I look in these photos! (Try to cut my fringe)
- Appear on the red carpet for the opening of something (Open up a bill I can't afford to pay)
- Indulge in a liquorice tea and one minute square of dark chocolate as a 'naughty treat' (Wish I could afford a block of chocolate).

Maybe I should put on my resume in bold font, *I'm a middle-aged woman with limited education and no money for expensive haircuts and colouring, and I mostly wear second-hand clothes.* She stifled a giggle as she put the magazine back in the rack, thinking she must remember to tell Rosie about the article.

When she got home, she turned on the radio to hear her new adversary, the Federal Treasurer, in full swing discussing superannuation. She got the gist of what he was saying, which was that retirees should be encouraged to top up their superannuation savings. Rachel couldn't even imagine a future in which that was a possibility, besides which she had more pressing concerns.

She had to call Energy Australia and beg for an extension.

Again.

Chapter Three

Nothing can prepare you for the agony of loneliness. When you're busy and surrounded by people, having some 'alone' time was a luxury. Rachel had come across the phrase in a magazine from the library. A beautiful blonde woman with three equally photogenic young children along with her clean-skinned, chiselled husband was pictured alongside an article where the woman (a busy 'influencer') was bemoaning her lack of 'me' time.

'The other night, I ran myself a bath, poured in my favourite bath oil, lit a few candles, and popped on an eye and face mask. I felt so guilty taking time out but it's so important us mums look after ourselves,' she gushed.

I used a candle the other night, too, when the power was turned off because I couldn't pay the bill.

Rachel could go for days without speaking to anyone. When she was out she was just a face in the crowd, a nobody. The library was her haven; sometimes a nod here and a hello there was all that was required to remind her that she was still alive. She had long accepted that she may have to live without physical contact. However, very few people could go for long periods without interacting with others.

Rachel realised she wasn't the only one who felt lonely. She noticed it on people's faces all over the place. Old people walking down the street or sitting in shopping malls killing time. Other people who, for whatever reason, had found themselves alone and isolated. They hadn't planned to, they hadn't wanted to, it just happened — not everyone was surrounded by large loving families and a slew of close friends. Lockdown had exacerbated the situation for so many.

She got to know the local charities. One provided a full bag of groceries for ten dollars, while others provided a free hot meal. Everyone was friendly; nobody looked down on her or judged her for what she was wearing. When she visited these places, she knew she had reached a point of desperation; pride had no place when you're broke and hungry.

She noticed the same people.

Leah was a small, wiry woman about Rachel's age, with spiky hair, an eyebrow ring, tattoos, and two missing front teeth, and seemed to always be trailing a plastic bag almost as big as her. They'd only exchanged a few words over the past several months until one slow day when neither of them had anywhere they needed to be, and they paused outside the Salvation Army and by some unspoken agreement started walking down the street together, each carrying their precious cargo.

Listening to Leah's slightly gravelly voice, Rachel learnt that she had been abused as a teenager by her mother's boyfriend. Her mother refused to believe her, and she ended up on the streets. After years of drug use, she was once again trying to put her life back together.

Leah always had a guarded, frightened expression on her face, as if something horrible was about to happen. She now understood why. Leah's bravery in sharing her story must have taken a lot of guts.

She often thought about that.

She sometimes shared a joke with Lucas, a muscled beast of a young man with a scraggly beard, and a love of tattoos. But underneath Lucas was a sensitive soul and liked a joke. He would laughingly tease her for her love, of all things, cans of tuna.

Gary was a proud Gadigal man who had fallen on hard times.

Living hand to mouth was a great social leveller, cutting across class, gender, and race.

There was a banging in her head. It seemed to be getting louder. She slowly pried her eyes open. Oh, that banging. She put her hands over her ears, and opened her eyes again, slowly trying to wake up. She ached all over. The banging kept going.

'Rachel, Rachel, are you there?' a voice said.

It wasn't in her head; someone was at the door. Gingerly, she opened it to find Rima holding a thermos. She bustled in, leading Rachel back to bed. 'You sick, I hear you,' she said.

Rachel rubbed her eyes, struggling to remember. She recalled feeling cold and making herself a cup of coffee before climbing into bed, hoping to warm up. With a start, she also remembered vomiting. Her stomach felt very odd, she must have dozed off because it was dark outside, and she was even colder than before.

Rachel began to protest, 'I'm fine, I feel better...' Her voice faded as weakness overcame her and she leaned back gratefully against the worn pillow Rima had propped up.

Kind Rima had bought her a cup of hot, sweet tea and some biscuits. Rima poured some into a cup and convinced Rachel to drink the sugary goodness.

The tea had made her feel better, and Rima left half an hour later, confident her magical concoction had had the desired effect. Rachel slept all night and on and off all day the next day, and by the afternoon her head was clear, and her stomach settled.

Rachel was no fool; she knew exactly what had caused her illness. She had survived the last few weeks on two-minute noodles, sometimes with eggs and frozen vegetables mixed in, and the occasional banana.

Around dawn the next morning, Rachel took two buses to a large office block on a new business estate. She'd seen the casual cleaning jobs advertised on a community notice board in the shopping centre, had rung, and been told to present herself at seven am. By car, the journey would be no more than fifteen minutes or so, but due to the vagaries of transport in Sydney's west, it was two buses with a wait in between to get to her destination.

She was very thankful for the work, and there was a real satisfaction from doing physical work and seeing the place in better shape than how she and the other cleaners found it. She'd already calculated how much of her earnings would go towards rent and bills, with enough left over for a decent meal.

Rachel was used to the endless debates in her head:

> *Can I make the toothpaste last another few days? Will adding water to the soup make it last longer, allowing me to buy some Panadol?*

When she got home, she knocked on Rima's door.

'Rima, thank you for yesterday,' she said when the door opened revealing her neighbour holding a grizzling Jamal.

Rima brushed away Rachel's thanks, looking uncharacteristically distracted and annoyed.

'Are you okay?' Rachel asked her.

'They have no idea, how I supposed to do the work, when they change their mind, treat us like slaves,' she said angrily before launching into a fresh attack in her native tongue.

'Slow down, slow down, what's happened?'

Half an hour later, with some relaxing music on the radio, Jamal was happily playing with his toys at Rachel's feet, looking up at her every so often and waving. Next door, his mum was busily completing the sewing work she was now on a tight deadline to complete. From what Rachel could work out, whoever gave Rima the work didn't take 'no' for an answer and kept changing their requirements. Rachel chuckled to herself feeling some sympathy for the person on the receiving end of her friend's wrath which, when in full force, could be quite something.

Rachel heard her phone beep. A message from Rosie. Melbourne was going back into a three-day lockdown due to some COVID-19 cases in the community. Rachel responded with a sad face emoji as Jamal tired of his toys and scrambled onto her lap for a cuddle.

The COVID-19 lockdown in Sydney in March 2020 had been a hard time for many, Rachel included. She'd been two months into a job as a casual warehouse administration assistant for a large furniture company. She'd been enjoying it; she had mastered the computer system they used, and she'd enjoyed talking to people in the stores all around Australia. But covid had changed all that, the shops had to temporarily close in line with Government orders and she was let go.

She'd never forget the day she returned to her flat to find Rima and Ali waiting for her. Their English was improving, but they were still struggling, and understandably they were feeling overwhelmed by what was happening. They muddled through together, and she helped them with any paperwork they needed to complete (although, as she had quipped to Rosie, she wasn't sure how much help she was as it was 'government bureaucracy on steroids.')

They all learnt a new vocabulary.

Rima had looked petrified when Rachel told them a 'lockdown' was happening.

'Are they putting us in jail?' she cried out.

Isolation, contact tracers, testing, masks, bubbles. They shared food and supported each other. Rosie had appointed herself a lockdown specialist (after going through it in Melbourne) so Rachel would receive text messages with the occasional sensible advice and often, completely useless information and funny memes to cheer her up.

As well as Rima and her family, she got to know others in the little block of flats. If anything, the pandemic brought a lot of people closer, the community rallying around each other. Old Mr Quan would sometimes poke his wizened face out the door as she was passing. His wife was bedridden; a parade of carers helped him look after her. They had been married for more than sixty years, he proudly told her one day, showing her a photo of their wedding day in Guangzhou in China. She sometimes picked up some shopping for him.

A Sudanese family was on the other side of the Quan's. Their boys loved playing soccer; their mother Naelia said to Rachel they normally spent more time at the park than at home.

'Why wasn't I blessed with a daughter?' she would say with a mocking shake of her head, then laugh uproariously.

Everyone was affected by COVID-19 in some way, and Rachel became a bit of a go-to person for people whose first language was not English. She didn't mind. She enjoyed assisting others, and it wasn't as if she didn't have the time...

Her knee was throbbing the next morning. She had fallen down some stairs a few years ago and landed heavily on her left knee. The doctor at the local medical centre bandaged it, and she'd been bedridden for a few days. He'd suggested physiotherapy, but she'd never been able to afford it, instead opting for an anti-inflammatory cream when her budget allowed. Some days she didn't feel it, but other days the pain was excruciating. Today was one of those days.

She hobbled slowly to the op shop hoping to find a jumper. She'd put off spending the money but now she needed it. She was in luck, for eight dollars she got an old men's navy-blue jumper, quite thick, and while there was a big hole in one of the sleeves, she was quite sure she could darn it, and no one would notice.

As she walked out of the shop, she noticed Leah sitting at a bus stop a little further down the road. She sat motionless, swaying slightly, with the ever-present big plastic bag at her feet. As Rachel got closer, she wondered if Leah was asleep.

'Leah?' said Rachel.

'Oh, hi,' Leah said looking up at her.

'Are you all right?'

'Yeah, yeah, I'm fine, just a little tired,' she said. Leah didn't look good. Her hair was matted, and she had grime on her cheek.

Rachel took a seat. 'I just got this jumper from the Red Cross shop,' she said as she unzipped her handbag and handed it to Leah who stared at it dull-eyed like she had never seen one before.

Noticing Leah was shivering, she suddenly asked, 'I live close by, would you like to come and have a cup of tea at my place?'

Leah contemplated the invitation as if she'd just been asked out to dinner and had to consult her busy schedule. 'That would be nice, thanks,' she finally said.

Chapter Four

Settled on the couch with a mug of tea each, Rachel felt Leah relaxing, some colour appearing on her face, although she still seemed to be shivering.

'Any news on the job front?' asked Rachel.

'Nup. It's hard, isn't it?' said Leah.

Rachel tried not to stare at her. She was so thin, and it was obvious life had not been kind to her. It was written all over her pinched face.

'I might have a chance at another rehab course though,' Leah said interrupting her thoughts.

'That's great Leah, I hope it works out,' Rachel said, the words sounding hollow amongst such obvious struggle and hardship.

They started to talk about other things, the weather, the local op shop, the traffic noise.

A knock on the door interrupted their conversation.

'Sorry, sorry Rachel, she wanted to show you her apple.' Rima was unsuccessfully trying to control Amira who was reaching up to Rachel, 'yapple, yapple!'

'It's fine Rima, come in. Oh, my Amira, who's got a big apple then,' said Rachel as she scooped her up into her arms, Amira's sticky fingers (the ones she used to wrap her mum and dad around) reaching out to grab Rachel's hair. Spotting Leah, the little girl thrust her arm towards her, 'yapple, yapple.'

Leah immediately tensed, her body rigid.

Rima reappeared, carrying a packet of biscuits that she offered to Rachel and Leah.

Rachel plopped Amira down on the floor, where she was instantly enthralled by Leah's green thongs. She continued to touch them before smiling and glancing up at Leah who seemed to have frozen, her hands tightly clutching her mug of tea.

Leah's eyes welled up as a large tear fell down her cheek. Rachel glanced at Rima before she softly inquired, 'Do you have children, Leah?'

Leah said nothing, her odd, closed expression a sign that the conversation was over.

Rima hoisted Amira on her shoulder, her daughter still yelling 'yapple, yapple' at Rachel and Leah, and closed the door.

'Leah, where are you living?' asked Rachel impulsively. 'As you can see, it's not much, but if you needed a place for a couple of nights,' she continued when she received no response.

'No, I'm fine,' Leah said.

Rachel didn't seem convinced.

'Honestly, it's okay, but I have to go.' Rachel showed Leah out, watching her until she was out of sight.

Leah stuffed her hands in her pockets as she walked along the street, a light drizzle falling. Her head was filled with images of little Amira; she had pulled on her heartstrings, triggered something. Her little arms stretched out, the cheeky grin, the dimples.

One Sunday, Rachel took the train to visit her mother.

When her mother got ill and couldn't look after herself, Rachel quit her job and moved in with her. It was hard; their roles were completely reversed. At times, she had to treat her mother as a child – helping her get to the toilet, bathing her, feeding her. She liked it best when her mother had enough energy and spirit left to argue with her — 'Rachel, I like my eggs boiled a little longer; Rachel, that doesn't belong there'.

Often, the arguments left them both exhausted and in tears. 'Don't treat me like an idiot, I'm still your mother!'

Rachel felt very lonely and isolated. She didn't get to catch up with the few friends she did have. She missed working. Her world shrunk to just her mum, the doctor's surgery, the pharmacist, the supermarket.

She didn't regret it, no matter how difficult it was. Her mother needed her, and she was not about to let her down.

Rachel had no choice but to place her mother in a nursing home after her mind continued to deteriorate. The cost had completely depleted their meagre savings. Rachel had been unable to pay the rent and had to move on.

Rachel's father abandoned her and her mother when she was four, with barely a backward glance. It would not be an exaggeration to say Rachel's mother never recovered from the pain of unrequited love. Mary, who married the strong, muscular Len when she was eighteen, became pregnant with Rachel only two years later. Heartbroken and rejected, as a single mother she had little choice but to take a series of cleaning jobs, eventually completing a secretarial course and finding more stable office work.

Money was tight. Mary worked hard to put food on the table. She became an expert at finding the best bargains and making meals stretch. She made many of her and Rachel's clothes. There was little money for extras, like school excursions or holidays away. Rachel never felt she was deprived in any way, although there were times when she wished she had a mum and dad and that they weren't always short of money. Some of her classmates would make fun of her when she couldn't afford to go on a school excursion, or even buy her lunch from the school canteen. She'd eat her Devon sandwiches, watching enviously as the other kids tucked into mouth-watering sausage rolls and chips.

She felt guilty when she felt that way. She loved her mum and knew she worked hard and did her best for her. As she grew up and observed other mothers interacting with their daughters, she sometimes felt her mum was detached, maybe at times unemotional. But she was always there for her and that was all that mattered.

Her mum's life was one of routine — home, her job, the occasional night out with people from her work. Rachel never asked her whether she was lonely; she suspected she was but would never admit it.

If Rachel thought about it, it was like she was turned off by men altogether. When Rachel was a teenager, she remembered her mum going out with a couple of blokes. They had seemed quite keen but they never lasted. She always gave them the flick.

'Why? What happened this time?' she'd ask.

The answer was always the same. 'You can't trust men, Rachel, we're better off just the two of us.'

Rachel had an inkling her mother still viewed her father through rose-coloured glasses because according to her, no one ever measured up to 'her Len'.

One night, teenage hormones pulsating through her body, she screamed, 'He isn't coming back, he left us!' Her mother had stayed in her room for hours crying. Rachel never forgave herself for that. She just wanted her to be happy, not pining after someone who had broken her heart and deserted her. It was at that moment Rachel knew she had no interest in meeting her father, even if she had known where he was.

When Rachel arrived at the nursing home, her mother was sitting in her favourite chair, dressed in the thick pink dressing gown she remembered from childhood, her watery blue eyes fixed on Rachel.

'Hello Rachel, is your father with you?' she'd ask.

It was always a long train ride home.

'Anyway, I thought I'd tell you,' Leah said looking dead straight ahead.

Rachel had gotten used to the way Leah confided in her. Unexpected. Without notice. One moment they were talking about something as innocuous as their favourite chocolate, the next Leah would reveal another layer of herself. The only tell-tale sign was she would often rub her arms, scratching at something that wasn't there.

Since Leah's first visit to the flat, they'd seen each other a few times. Leah was sleeping on a friend's couch for a few weeks but seemed to enjoy spending time at Rachel's unit, and Rachel loved the company. Sometimes Rima and the kids joined them.

She now knew that after running away from home when she was sixteen, after her mother's boyfriend assaulted her, she'd lived in Kings Cross, a haven for Sydney's homeless youth in the 1980s. She moved around a lot, staying wherever she could.

'That was when it all began,' Leah told Rachel a few weeks ago. She'd gotten involved with the wrong crowd, scrounging for alcohol, drugs, and whatever else she could get her hands on.

Now she looked at her friend, still staring dead ahead, refusing to make eye contact.

The air felt thick between them. Rachel knew better than to reach out and comfort her. Sometimes she was prickly, would often reject a comforting arm. Looking at the defiant silhouette this was one of those times.

'It must be very hard for you.'

Leah's face was pallid. 'I wasn't a very good mother. I tried; I did. But —'

'What about the father?'

Leah's shoulders relaxed slightly, and she turned to Rachel. 'Jimmy was all right at first. He was working at a mechanics; I was at TAFE. But Jimmy was always stoned — oh, I had my fair share, but he took it to another level — he stopped turning up for work and got the sack. I was about to dump him when I found out I was pregnant.'

'So, you stayed with him?'

'My first mistake was to trust Jimmy and to think that he could change. He begged me not to leave him. Said we could be family.'

She paused.

'Jake was born in 1985. At first, Jimmy had been true to his word. He worked hard, was a real dad. I used to love seeing him cradle Jake while I made the dinner, he'd sing him silly rhymes he made up.'

She took a deep breath. 'I was an idiot, I thought that maybe one day we'd make it out of public housing, that we'd have a place of our own. When I had Natalie I thought we'd be a family.'

Tears fell down Leah's cheek.

'He would just get stoned and do nothing, sit around all day making stupid jokes, never did anything to help. I was the one stressing and worrying about how we would make ends meet with the benefit money and put food on the table.'

She paused to blow her nose.

'One day Jimmy announced he was leaving. He couldn't do the "family thing" he said, using air quotes as if I was incapable of understanding what he was saying,' Leah scoffed.

'I loved those kids, Rachel. I didn't know I could love like that, I tried so hard. But—'

Rachel tentatively reached out and put an arm around Leah who was now openly sobbing. She could guess the rest; she knew enough about Leah's struggles, her relapses.

The next morning Rachel attended a workshop put on by one of the community job support organisations. She had already attended a couple and not only were they quite helpful but meeting other job seekers helped alleviate the sense of isolation and loneliness she felt. It was, however, a bitter double-edged sword: as the months flew by with no permanent job in sight, her sense of failure was strong, and seeing the same faces each time made her realise she wasn't the only one.

When she walked into the little room at the Community Centre, written across the whiteboard in big letters was 'AGE DISCRIMINATION IS ILLEGAL'. Topical, Rachel thought, as she glanced at the handful of other jobseekers, roughly the same age as her.

She sat next to Robert who she had met at other workshops. Robert was about five years older than her, widowed with three adult children. He had been made redundant from the public service. Like her, he had applied for hundreds of jobs but had not been able to find steady work.

A young woman wearing a green patterned dress entered the room. She introduced herself as Clare Bristow, an employment rights lawyer and said she was going to help them understand the rights they had as jobseekers. Well, she looks helpful and approachable, thought Rachel, as she settled down to listen.

An hour later Rachel's head was spinning. Given her experience, she knew she'd been on the receiving end of discrimination, but she had no idea how widespread it was.

Robert told the group about when he went for an interview for a call centre position, and the interviewer had said, 'If I knew you were this old, I wouldn't have interviewed you.'

A quiet stocky bloke called Neville joined in. 'I've worked in furniture removal; I was a carpenter and a brick paver. I rang a bloke a while back who was looking for a casual paver, and he asked how old I was. When I told him I was fifty-seven, he laughed and said thanks for calling.'

'Look at me,' said Neville showing his muscly arms to the group. 'I could easily have done the job.'

Everyone was aghast, except Clare.

'Sadly, this happens way too frequently,' she said to her by-now-despondent class.

'No one is interested in what you can bring to a company,' said Lin sitting on the other side of Rachel. 'They don't ask what you have been doing previously, they just say, *Well, it has been a long time since you've been working in that area,* and forget about you.'

During a break for coffee, she found herself standing next to Robert.

He told her he had an interview the next day. 'It's only part-time, but I'm trying to be positive.'

'Is it the public service?' she asked.

'No, it's for a technology company, to write their sales tender documents.' He studied his watch for a few moments. 'I'm embarrassed in front of the kids, not being able to tell them I'm working and earning money.'

She struggled to find the right words to comfort him and said, 'I'm sure they understand,' which to her ears sounded pitifully inadequate.

He smiled. 'They do, they're great. But enough about me, how are you doing?'

'I'm alright, but it's hard, you know. I'm not even close to getting anything.' She told him about her run of job rejections and disastrous interviews.

Robert didn't come out with any of the usual platitudes, instead he asked her questions about herself. Later, when she mulled over their conversation, she realised he'd done it deliberately to stop her fixating on her situation, diverting her attention.

'I left school at sixteen and was doing a hairdressing apprenticeship. I was at TAFE one day a week, and it was great at first, shampooing, conditioning, removing colours, helping with perms. You name it, I did it. Of course, there was all the floor sweeping and cleaning basins, but I loved it.'

'What happened?' asked Robert taking a sip of his coffee then grimacing at the bitter taste.

'After a while, the manager just stopped training me. I tried talking to her about it, but she just snapped at me, telling me I should be grateful for the job in the first place. After that, she barely spoke to me and when she did it was to yell at me or tell me I had to work through my break.'

'You were bullied,' he said quietly.

'Yeah. It was a bit better when a new manager came in but by then I'd had enough. I'd left school at sixteen,' she shrugged. 'I got an office job in a small manufacturing place, and...' Rachel shrugged her shoulders again. 'But I'm a hard worker, I just need a chance,' she said fiercely.

As they stood together, Rachel stole a glance at Robert, taking in the tall well-groomed man, his open friendly face, the way his kind blue eyes matched his crisp checked shirt.

He must have felt her eyes on him, because at that moment he turned and smiled at her, and she felt herself blush.

'And I think you deserve a chance too, Rachel Farrowsworth,' he said his eyes holding hers for a moment before they made their way back to the group.

Clare was good. When she saw the despondent faces in front of her, she set about lifting the mood by getting the class to call out reasons why employers should hire older workers, which she then wrote on the whiteboard.

'Life experience,' said one.

'We've been around, we know what works,' said someone else.

'We've got the skills — we just need a go.'

'We know how to work hard.'

'We're not going to leave.'

'I've raised four kids on my own,' said a woman up the back of the room. 'Don't tell me I don't know how to multi-task.' Everyone laughed, including Clare.

'It's true,' said Robert looking around at the group. 'Everything we've said,' he stretched his arms out, 'all this experience is worth something. Someone will see the value in that, we just have to keep persevering.'

Everyone nodded, and Rachel looked at him admiringly thinking it was no wonder everyone liked him.

Afterwards, they all lingered outside, reluctant to get back to the day-to-day grind of searching for work.

'Do you still go to the library?' a voice next to her asked.

It was Lin. A qualified accountant, she too had been made redundant. She lived with her eldest son and his wife, but Rachel knew from previous conversations it was a cramped tiny unit and Lin wanted to have her own place again. Lin was born in Malaysia.

She and her husband migrated to Australia in the 1980s and they both worked hard. Her husband died of a heart attack about five years ago.

'Yep, all the time, Lin,' Rachel replied.

They arranged to catch up and exchanged phone numbers.

Looking through her bag for a tissue, Rachel felt grateful for the work these community organisations did. A while ago she attended a workshop where she learnt how to access government services information and payments. She, like everyone else there, felt there was no way that they could have done it without help. Having the right ID, creating Customer Reference Numbers, accounts, logins. It was a minefield. Rachel didn't want to be the government's responsibility, she felt strongly about that, but when it was the last resort what option did she have? She always made sure she thanked the people who ran these workshops — many people like her didn't have a computer, and answering countless questions took patience!

Chapter Five

I look so old. No wonder no one will employ me.

Rachel slowly lowered her nail scissors. She was in the middle of the tricky business of cutting her fringe. It had grown right into her eyes, causing her to squint even more than she usually did.

She looked at herself with something close to disgust. Her mousey brown hair was lank and stringy, streaked with grey. She had dark circles under her eyes. Her skin was pale and greasy, the old acne scars visible.

Hearing a knock on the door, Rachel gasped as she opened it.

'Leah, are you okay, what happened?' A huge purple and black bruise snaked across Leah's swollen right eye and cheek.

Rachel pulled her into the unit, hugging her. She seemed even smaller and frailer than usual. She led her to a chair and hurried to make her a cup of tea.

'What happened Leah?' she repeated gently.

In a voice so faint Rachel had to lean forward to hear her, she learnt Leah had been staying at a house where any number of people seemed to bed down for a night. As always, she was vague about how she came to be staying there.

One night, there was a party.

'It was like a lot of parties I've been to. I was scared to be there because I've worked so hard to get this far. I didn't take any drugs, I swear, but it freaked me out,' said Leah.

There was a pause.

'I caught some guy going through my bag, looking for money I guess. I tried to grab my bag and he shoved me. I grabbed at it again and that's when he did this,' she said pointing to her poor face.

'You need to go to the police!'

Leah looked at Rachel with raised eyebrows. 'Rachel, look at me, do you think the police are going to care about an ex-junkie? And besides —'

'What?'

'It's not like I haven't done the same thing before to some other poor bugger.'

Rachel fixed her gaze on Leah. She looked past the pitted skin and nicotine-tainted fingers that matched her teeth. She saw a woman her age who'd been through so much in her life, who'd done things she wasn't proud of and lost her children in the process, who'd hit rock bottom and was doing her best to survive.

'Right, that's it,' Rachel said. 'You're staying here.'

They both looked around the room doubtfully.

'Okay, it will be a tight squeeze,' Rachel conceded, 'but we'll make it work. You can't go back to that place,' she said.

Leah had tears in her eyes. 'Thank you,' she said.

As usual Rima came to the rescue. She brought across a few old cushions and a blanket. All Leah had with her was a plastic bag of some of her things, which fitted neatly in the corner of the lounge room.

With her legs hanging over the end of the couch (despite her short stature), Leah pounded the cushion into shape, hoping to soften the blow of the couch springs that dug into her back. It didn't matter, she thought as she sank gratefully into the warm blanket. The room was pitch black. She could hear the traffic outside, but everything else was quiet.

She'd only stopped shaking an hour ago. Despite having spent some time together over the past few months — even though they couldn't be more different — she wasn't sure what she was expecting when she showed up unexpectedly at Rachel's.

Rachel was not like anyone Leah would ever have hung out with before. She shuddered as she remembered some of the people she had spent time with. People who were only concerned with themselves, who would go to any length to get their next hit.

She had been one of them.

Leah turned over, her legs tucked close to her body and settled down again. Her cheek throbbed from where the punch had connected. *At least I don't have to go back there again*, she thought thankfully before falling asleep.

An animated Amira arrived to see 'Auntie Rachel's friend' early the next day. Rima and Ali laughed as their bossy daughter told Leah where she lived and that she *must* come and visit her.

'You get some rest and look after yourself now, and we'll see you soon.' They pressed Leah's hand as they took their excitable daughter home, leaving Leah feeling wobbly with gratitude and emotion.

Rosie was cautiously supportive of the arrangement. She had nothing against Leah — it was just that she wanted Rachel to concentrate on herself. She knew Rachel's kind nature had been taken advantage of before and didn't want to see her friend hurt again.

A week or so later they were able to get a cheap second-hand mattress from a charity shop. After the first night, Leah declared it was the best night's sleep she'd ever had.

Leah was fastidiously tidy. The little flat remained cold and dark but it had never been so clean.

She loved changing her hair colour. She'd buy a cheap temporary hair colour spray whenever she could. Now it was a bright green, which Rachel had to admit, suited her.

Rachel was intrigued by the things people covet when they were short on money. It was a fresh, sweet-smelling bar of soap and shower gel for Rachel. For Rima, a brightly coloured cushion made her day. Rachel was surprised when she discovered that Leah would often look longingly at dainty old-fashioned teacups and saucers in the op shops she frequented.

Meanwhile, as the household settled into its new routines, Rachel had another telephone interview for a sales administration role. She must have done well as they'd asked her to complete an online clerical aptitude test.

Her excitement quickly turned to panic.

'I don't own a computer,' she said despairingly to Fiona, the recruitment agent.

'Oh. Perhaps you can borrow one?'

Yes, thought Rachel, sticking her tongue out at the phone, why didn't I think of that, Leah and Rima both have top of the range iPads...

'Oh, hang on, I can use a computer at the library?' she said remembering that she was well familiar with the library's computer set up.

Rachel wrote everything down Fiona told her. Book computer. Email Fiona to tell her the day and time. The test would then be emailed to her at that time, and she would have thirty minutes to complete it.

She arrived at the library fifteen minutes before the appointed time. To her surprise, she wasn't nervous. It was as if she was so thrilled to have made it through the telephone interview that her nerves had disappeared.

Rachel greeted Helen cheerfully and then logged onto the computer allocated to her. At ten am precisely the test arrived in her in-box, and she clicked on it.

This clerical ability test will assess your attention to detail, basic maths, filing and verbal skills. The test consists of two sub-tests:

1. *Attention to Detail*

2. *Ability Test*

When you are ready to start, click 'Begin' to see instructions for the first sub-test.

Rachel was feeling more than ready, and she began the test.

Halfway through the test, she was feeling good. She had read every question carefully and nothing was proving too difficult. She moved confidently to the next section which was some maths questions. Having calculated the answer she clicked on the box in which to type the correct answer.

Nothing happened.

She tried again. Nothing.

Rachel moved the mouse around as Helen had once shown her to do. She checked the cursor. It wasn't moving.

Rachel looked up, trying to see if Helen or any of the other library staff were free to come and help her, but there was a queue of people at the front desk. The other computer users were engrossed in what they were doing or were wearing headphones, and in any case, she was too embarrassed to bother them.

She looked back at the screen. Still nothing. It was like it had frozen. She wondered if she could get back to the previous question and try again. But no, that didn't work either. Looking at the time on the computer she was horrified to see the half an hour allowed for the test was nearly up. She pressed the Enter key furiously. Nothing.

Suddenly the screen sprang back to life. Hooray, thought Rachel. She quickly answered another two maths questions and was about to tackle the next when a box suddenly appeared on the screen: *This test has expired.*

Rachel sat back in her chair defeated, close to tears.

When she got home all she wanted to do was curl up and forget about the morning. Rima was visiting with Amira and Jamal, and normally the sight of the children cheered her up. Especially as Amira had declared Leah her new best friend and was happily trying to tie a ribbon around tufts of her spiky hair.

'You need to ring her,' said Leah after Rachel had told them what happened.

'I just...I...Oh, what's the point?'

'Now come on,' said Leah, 'you're the one who is always telling me not to give up.' Thanks to Rachel's encouragement Leah had got a casual cleaning job at the same company where Rachel picked up the occasional shift. It wasn't much but it was a start.

Leah convinced her. She could be quite bossy, thought Rachel, even with a bright red ribbon tied around her head.

In the end Fiona the recruiter wasn't at her desk and Rachel was forced to leave a message. It didn't matter, thought Rachel, she knew she wasn't going to get the job.

The next day when she logged into her email, she was proven right. An email was waiting for her: Fiona was sorry she'd had computer problems, but they'd received a high volume of applications and had made a short list of who they wanted to interview. Fiona had wished her good luck.

No matter what I do, no matter how hard I try, I just can't win.

Chapter Six

Rachel and Leah had gotten into the habit of taking a mug of tea and sitting by the lounge room window after whatever dinner they managed to scratch together.

'We can pretend we're sitting on a balcony with a view of Sydney Harbour,' said Leah.

Rachel shoved up the window. For months it had been sticking but she deftly opened it, only to be greeted by a blast of car horns and exhaust fumes.

'Well, we can dream,' said Leah drily as they both laughed.

Rachel looked at Leah. Her eyes were brighter, and while she was still painfully thin, she was looking less frail by the day.

'You're looking so much better,' she said.

'I feel it. I'm going to meetings regularly, and it's nice going to bed and not having to keep on guard for the whole night.' As well as couch surfing, Rachel suspected that Leah had spent time on the streets recently.

'The work helps too,' she added. The casual cleaning jobs, along with going to her meetings regularly was giving her days some structure.

Rachel stretched as she looked around the flat. They'd been able to inject some little splashes of colour into the room — a cushion, a bright coloured tea towel, a vibrant yellow bedspread (it amazed Rachel the quality of goods some people donated to charity shops), a couple of green mugs. They'd also replaced one of the light bulbs with a brighter one; it had made a huge difference. One day Rachel thought when they *both* had permanent work, they'd be able to afford a heater, but until then, they made do with huddling under a huge bright blue blanket Leah got from the Salvation Army years ago and never parted with.

Rachel started to laugh.

'What?' said Leah.

Rachel pointed to her head.

'Oh, this,' Leah laughed too, pulling a green ribbon from her head, courtesy of Amira's demand to play hairdressers earlier.

'She adores you,' Rachel said.

Leah sipped her tea. 'Did you ever want kids?'

Rachel gave the impression she was giving the question some thought.

'You don't have to answer,' said Leah.

'No, it's okay. No, I didn't,' she said. If Leah was surprised by the abruptness of the response, she didn't say anything.

'Never met the right man?' said Leah.

'Something like that,' she said before changing the subject.

Rachel walked down the street thinking it was nice to have something to look forward to — she was meeting Lin after she went to the library. Thinking of Lin made her feel even more perplexed about the current job situation; Lin was qualified, had years of experience and was continually told she was over-qualified or wasn't quite the right fit (she was adamant that on many occasions a mixture of racism and ageism was at play: 'they don't like the way I look,' she would say bluntly). If Lin with her qualifications couldn't get a job what did that mean for the rest of us, thought Rachel despondently.

She thought about Robert as she walked — it had been a long time since she had thought about a man — and how much she enjoyed talking to him at the workshop they'd both attended.

As she meandered through the shopping centre she noticed again how the suburb was changing. She'd read about it online. More and more people and families, unable to afford property closer to the Sydney CBD, were moving further out. She'd seen a lot of new houses being built. The house prices astounded her. Even the shops were looking different. She worried about what it would mean for the currently cheap rent she paid.

Rachel eyed some of the young people around her. Groomed to perfection. Their expensive sneakers, fancy phones, and earbuds. She wondered what it was like to be that age in 2021 and be able to buy things at a whim — drinks at a bar here, dinner at a restaurant there, a new dress, a holiday.

I don't even want that, she thought fiercely.

I just want enough to not be constantly worried about making ends meet.

When Rachel got home later that afternoon, she could hear crying coming from inside Rima and Ali's flat. She hesitated at the door not knowing whether she should knock and check everything was okay. It could be a private matter, thought Rachel, I'll leave it. At that moment, the door opened, and Rima's tear-stained face peered out at her.

'Rima, what is it?' said Rachel worriedly.

'Oh Rachel, I've been waiting for you. Come in, come in.'

Rachel followed Rima into the flat, noticing how unusually quiet it was. Rachel gasped. Ali was sitting at the dining table, nursing a black eye, swollen mouth, and bruised arms. He grimaced as he looked up at Rachel.

'What happened?'

'He was attacked, his phone and money stolen,' said Rima sitting down next to Ali, then immediately getting up, wringing her hands as she stood next to her husband.

Ali had finished his shift and had been walking down an alleyway near the station when he was set upon by two men. He tried to fight back but to no avail.

'Did you go to the police?' asked a shocked Rachel.

Ali and Rima exchanged glances. Rachel understood from previous conversations they did not trust the police because of things that happened to them in Syria. She had told them many times that things were different in Australia, but she had had to accept that Ali and Rima were victims of the cruelty they had witnessed, and were not going to change their beliefs anytime soon.

'I think you should,' she continued. 'I understand how difficult it is for you, but others are willing to help.'

Rima, her tears now turning to anger, did not look so sure.

Ali put his arm around his wife and looked at Rachel. 'They called me names, swore at me, said they'd come after me again.' He suddenly looked tired and older than his years. 'I know that was probably just talk but I just want to forget the whole thing.' He gestured at Rima pointedly.

She nodded. 'I understand,' she said although in truth she didn't. If it had happened to her, she knew what she would do. 'Is there anything I can do?'

Rima stood up. 'It's a big favour, but we wondered if you could look after Amira tonight. We don't want her to see her Papa's face like this, we're hoping the swelling will go down by the morning but—'

'Of course, think nothing of it,' she said.

Rima was looking fired up again. 'Everyone is so nice here. But today reminded me that not everyone is so welcoming to people like *us*,' she said bitterly, her eyes hard.

Rachel hugged her tightly. 'Look after Ali, we'll talk later,' she said looking down at her friend.

Little Amira was ecstatic with the arrangements.

Rachel and Leah had never been so tired in their lives. They played all her games and read all her stories until she fell asleep in Rachel's bed. Rachel awoke a few hours later and sprung to her feet when she realised Amira was nowhere to be found. She dashed into the living room to see Amira, her tubby arms spread above her head, sound asleep in the middle of Leah's mattress with a snoring Leah on the floor next to her. Thinking Rima would have a fight on her hands the next night trying to convince Amira to sleep in her own bed, she went back to bed chuckling.

Rosie was on the phone to her explaining about influencers. She had ditched Oprah and was now worshipping a twenty-something woman who had won some sort of reality TV show, and according to Rosie everything she posted should be followed verbatim. It wasn't making much sense to Rachel, but she knew better than to challenge Rosie mid-flow.

'She has more than 200,000 followers, a whole lot of them are celebrities, and she starts every day with a quote. She says it helps her set up a positive mindset for the day, and it never lets her down!' gushed Rosie.

'What was today's one then?' asked Rachel humouring her friend.

The sun is yours; the moon is yours; so why not rule the planet!... Rachel, you still there?'

'Yep, still here.'

'What do you think?'

'About what?'

'Rachel, the quote! Doesn't it just make perfect sense!'

Rachel giggled. 'No Rosie, it doesn't make any sense at all, and neither do you. I can't believe I'm saying this but I'm starting to miss my daily dose of Oprah!'

'Hmm, just you wait, you'll see, I'm going to text you each day's quote, it will make a real difference I bet you,' said Rosie in the face of her friend's predictable scepticism.

The next afternoon, her phone beeped. It was a message from Rosie.

'Um sorry (sad face emoji), I forgot to send this earlier!'

'It's never too early in the day to start planning your tomorrow!'

Rachel burst out laughing before sending a quick text: *Lucky you didn't send this yesterday, I'd be very disappointed.*

She was not surprised to receive an angry face emoji in return.

Meanwhile, her job-hunting was going nowhere. Her confidence was plummeting – jobs that months ago she would have applied for, she now second-guessed herself.

What's the point, I'm never going to even get an interview.

When they chatted later, Rosie told her, 'You have to keep applying.'

'What's the point?' she said obstinately. 'Do you know what happened to me the other day?'

Without waiting for an answer, she continued. 'I was out and got a call about an admin/reception job I'd applied for. They wanted to ask me a few questions before they decided who to bring in for an interview. You know what I'm like without my notes in front of me. Anyway, surprise surprise, it didn't go well. They weren't interested. And do you want to know the worst thing? I WAS SITTING IN BIRD POO ON A PARK BENCH!'

Rosie knew she had to proceed carefully when Rachel was in this state — normally they would have laughed about something like this.

'You will get a job, Rachel. Is it taking longer than we thought it would? Yes. Is it harder than we thought it would be? Definitely. But it will happen. You just have to keep going.'

'I'm so tired of it.'

'I know,' said Rosie softly. 'You've had it tough but you're doing so well, you can't stop applying, you can't give up.'

Rachel didn't respond.

'And Rachel,' Rosie continued, 'you have no choice.'

Rachel sensed something was bothering Leah. Their flat sharing was amazingly harmonious for two people who were used to being on their own and were now sharing a rather cramped space. Whether they needed to give each other space or whether they needed to lean on each other, they seemed to instinctively know what the other needed, and Rachel could tell that Leah's mind was often elsewhere.

A few days later, she returned from an early morning cleaning job, dumped her bag on the floor and found Leah sitting morosely on her mattress, a cup at her feet.

'Another cup of tea? That one looks cold,' she said.

Leah looked up, her face pale and tear stained.

'What is it, Leah?' said Rachel sitting down next to her. 'What's happened?'

'You remember how I told you my kids were in foster care?' said Leah, wiping her eyes. Rachel nodded.

'Well, they were eventually adopted by the foster parents,' she continued.

Rachel could hardly speak, imagining what that must have been like for Leah, the feelings of grief and loss she must have felt.

'It was the right thing to do. It's taken me years to accept it, but I couldn't look after them. They were raised by really good people,' said Leah.

'Did you ever see them?'

'There were supervised visits, but I was in and out of rehab so much, it wasn't always allowed,' said Leah. 'I regret all the years I've wasted. I missed out on so much.'

Rachel made them both a fresh cup of tea and sat back down. Leah handed her a piece of paper. She read it in silence and handed it back.

'I'm so sorry, Leah.'

Leah's daughter Natalie was now married and expecting her first child. Leah wanted to re-connect, see if she could play a role in her daughter's life and that of her future grandchild. However, Natalie saw things differently and did not want to have any relationship with her birth mother.

'I can't say I blame her,' said Leah. She started rubbing at her arm, then biting her nails, tell tale signs that Rachel knew meant she felt the opposite of what she said.

Privately Rachel thought differently, Leah had already paid the highest price for the mistakes she had made in the past.

'What about your son?' she asked.

'I haven't heard from him, he's living in the outback somewhere,' Leah said. 'I just thought...'

'What?'

'I'm not making excuses — I was a terrible mother who didn't deserve to be their mother when I was using. But I figured now that Natalie was an adult and about to have a kid, she'd give me another chance.' Leah defiantly wiped the tears from her face with her fist.

Chapter Seven

Never too late to change careers, the title screamed. Rachel was in the library and had picked up a magazine, one she wouldn't normally look at, about women who have swapped one successful career for another. Margie, a woman in her fifties who'd spent years working as a psychologist, was now training as a pastry chef; forty-five year old Rhonda was setting up her own floristry business after twenty years of teaching; and Patricia, tired of working in finance, was retraining as a massage therapist.

She roughly shoved the magazine back where she found it, not bothering to read about these smug women who exuded prosperity and success with their fashionable clothes and perfect smiles.

More rejection emails in her inbox just added to her mood.

When she got home, she walked into the kitchen, only to see Leah stuffing something into her pocket before turning around, looking furtive, her face red.

'What's that?' asked Rachel.

'Nothing,' said Leah edging into the living room.

'Then what's this?' she asked picking up a crumpled one hundred dollar note she had spied lying under the benchtop.

'I can explain,' said Leah, turning around.

'You better. Please tell me this has nothing to do with drugs, Leah?'

Leah hesitated.

'Oh Leah, we made a deal!'

'It's not what you think, I'm not using or dealing again, I promise. I'm done with all that.'

'Then where did you get the money from, and how much? And don't tell me it's none of my business because it is!'

'Five hundred dollars.'

Rachel gasped.

'It was owed to me Rachel, I promise!'

'Who owed it to you?'

'It's better you don't know—'

'Agghhhh, Leah!' She threw her hands in the air in frustration.

'Look, you have to trust me, this money was owed to me, and I got it back, that's all you need to know,' said Leah imploring Rachel to understand. 'Please don't kick me out,' she said desperately, her eyes wild.

Rachel knew she and Leah were an unlikely match, with nothing in common except the need to survive. But, as Rachel had discovered, relationships came in all shapes and sizes, and much to her (and she guessed Leah's) surprise they had become firm friends.

'I'm not going to kick you out, you're my friend. I want to trust you, but...it's not only me. What about Rima and the kids? They're here a lot, what happens if whoever you took this money from decides to come after you?'

'I told you, it's mine!'

'Okay, okay, I just hope the other person sees it like that.' Rachel held her hands up in defence.

Leah refused to meet her eye, instead saying, 'I thought I could help more with the bills.'

'We could have a slap-up steak!' she continued with a hesitant smile as if a hearty meal could appease her friend.

'Leah, I want to trust you,' Rachel repeated, 'but I don't want anything to do with this money. You've told me you're not using or dealing and that's all I need to know.'

Leah retreated to her mattress in the corner, while Rachel went into her bedroom, both upset at the tension that now existed in their small space.

Later she would remember she said, 'I want to trust you' not 'I do trust you.'

The week after, Rachel was in the library using the computer when an article caught her eye: *Local businessman Geoffrey Miles kills partner then himself in suspected murder-suicide.*

Time stopped. The air seemed thicker. She could see and hear people around her, but everything was fuzzy like she was underwater. Her hands were clammy. She cried out. Then everything went black.

Helen's concerned face swam in and out of focus. 'Rachel, there that's better, you must have fainted. Take your time, breathe slowly.'

Rachel looked around her. Or rather she looked up, as she seemed to be on the floor. She had attracted quite a group of nosy onlookers, drawn to a small bit of drama in their otherwise mundane day.

'What happened?' croaked Rachel in a voice that didn't seem to be hers. Suddenly she remembered — the article! She felt her heart quicken and she clutched Helen's hand.

Once Helen was sure no ambulance was needed, she settled Rachel in the small library office, got her a cup of tea and said she'd be back to check on her shortly. Helen was convinced she fainted because she skipped breakfast and Rachel was happy to let her believe that.

As Rachel stood on her still unsteady legs, Helen insisted on walking her to a taxi.

'Helen, really, no, I'll just walk home,' she protested, knowing she couldn't afford a taxi but also wondering how she was going to walk the short way home when her legs didn't seem to be working properly.

Helen, being Helen, intuitively knew why Rachel was protesting and took no notice. She hailed a taxi, gave the driver some money, and hugged Rachel, telling her to go home and rest.

Her hand was shaking as she unlocked the front door. She glanced at her neighbour's door, for once glad little Amira hadn't been waiting for her. She didn't think she could cope with those huge innocent eyes and toothy smile that morning.

She tried drinking a glass of water, but it wouldn't go down. She ran to the toilet, holding the bowl and dry retching. When she'd finished and with shaking hands, she rang Rosie.

Chapter Eight

When Rachel was thirty-two, she worked in a call centre for a large electrical and furniture retailer. It wasn't a bad job. She'd sit in her little pod and take calls regarding the delivery of goods or account queries.

She liked the neatness of her pod. She kept her desk clear of rubbish; her pens, highlighters, and stick-it notes carefully stacked beside her scrupulously clean computer and headset. Her mug (pink, emblazoned with *Life Is Better with Coffee and Chocolate*) close at hand.

One Monday morning, she was about to make her first call to sort out a delivery problem from the weekend, when the phone rang.

'Orders and deliveries, Rachel Farrowsworth speaking.'

'Rachel, it's Geoffrey, how are you?'

Her stomach did a slight summersault.

'Oh hi, Geoffrey, I'm good. You?'

'Well, it's Monday and I have a desk of problems to sort out. Get up to much on the weekend?'

'Um, no not really. Well, a few things, but you know, nothing too exciting,' she mumbled.

'I bet that's not true, not someone like you, Rachel,' Geoffrey said smoothly in response. 'You must be beating them off with a stick.'

Despite her shyness, Rachel giggled.

With that, their conversation went back to work matters and trying to resolve how a television (meant for a customer in Manly) was sitting in the lounge room of a customer in Liverpool who was still waiting for her new refrigerator and demanding compensation for her spoilt food.

Rachel had started to look forward to speaking to Geoffrey, the manager of one of the biggest stores. She'd first spoken to him months ago, and over time they moved from purely work calls to chats about other things. His calls had slowly become a highlight of her week.

She was nervous the first time she knew she was going to meet him. There was a big staff meeting one Wednesday and most of the store managers were coming into the office. Before the meeting, she went to the ladies. She'd spent an hour that morning deciding what she would wear and had chosen a new blouse for the occasion, a floral pattern of red and orange, with a bright red lipstick to match. Paired with a tailored black skirt, she was pleased with what she saw in the mirror. Her brown hair was shiny and bouncy from a weekend cut.

As she was walking back to the pod, she noticed her colleagues talking to a man she hadn't seen before. He was about the same height as her, perhaps a bit shorter. He had neat brown hair, flecks of grey visible. He seemed to be telling a joke, judging by the faces of her colleagues. He looked nice, she thought.

'Well, what do you think I did? I had another beer of course!' the man said, her colleagues laughing along. My goodness, thought Rachel, even Margie, their tyrant of a supervisor, was hanging off every word.

As Rachel walked up to the pod, one of her colleagues called out, 'Hey Rachel, this is Geoffrey. Geoffrey, Rachel.' Introductions made, the rest of the team gradually dispersed either back to their desks or to the big conference room.

'Rachel, nice to put a face to the name,' Geoffrey said shaking her hand. 'I feel like I already know you,' he winked at her. She wished she had control of her face, which she was sure at that very moment was red from blushing.

Geoffrey lowered his voice, 'and you're even prettier than I thought.'

Over the next few months, Rachel finally felt like part of a club. One that she had wanted to belong to for so long but never felt she would.

She had a boyfriend!

On their first date, Geoffrey had taken her to an Italian restaurant. She had been amazed there was even a second date as she was so nervous from the time he picked her up on that first evening together, she felt like she barely uttered a word during the whole night. Again, she had dithered over what she should wear. A dress? No, too dressy, too formal. Rosie was consulted and together they agreed her new blue jeans and a bright floral top would work.

Geoffrey had done most of the talking. She was happy to sit and listen, basking in the knowledge she was on a date. She was sure everyone in the restaurant could tell. Her smile seemed brighter, her heart rate faster.

Later, much later, Rachel would remember small details. His small pudgy sweaty hands, and how even at that first dinner he ordered for her and dominated the conversation.

Over the next few months, Rachel fell head over heels in love. She caught herself smiling at odd moments; singing love songs when she was getting ready to go out. When she bought a new dress, she bought it with Geoffrey in mind. She spent her days counting the hours until she would next see him and when she wasn't with him, she spent hours thinking about the last time they had seen each other.

It took her a long time to realise she had fallen in love with the thought of being in love. With the concept of love — what everyone wants but not everyone gets.

The first time they slept together, they were on a weekend away staying at a small bed and breakfast in the country. It had been a picture-perfect day, Rachel remembered. They had gone for a walk, had a long lunch in a local pub. At dinner that night in the hotel, they were one of four couples, all enjoying a romantic escape. She had bought a new nightie, soft pink, with matching underwear; tiny, embroidered rosebuds sewed into the delicate material. After a few glasses of champagne, she was eager for them to go back to their cosy bedroom with the subtle lighting and spa bath.

Rachel lost her virginity in the back seat of a car with Kevin, a boy she had vaguely known at high school who she ran into years later. By the time she was twenty-three, her virginity felt like a millstone around her neck, and she was determined to divest herself of it and Kevin seemed as good a candidate as anyone, but the awkward back seat fumbling was far removed from the fireworks and quivering orgasms she had read about. As Kevin boasted enough about his experience, she reasoned it must have been her fault and assumed there was something wrong with her.

The Egyptian cotton sheets on the four-poster bed were an improvement on the vinyl seats of the old Falcon, but the result was much the same. She was left feeling empty and deflated. Geoffrey didn't seem to notice, he huffed and puffed and came quickly, then kissed her on the lips before snoring his way into the next day.

After six months of going out, Geoffrey asked Rachel to move in with him. He had taken her to the Italian restaurant they had gone to on their first date. After their tiramisu (something Geoffrey introduced her to), he asked her.

'What did you say?' Rosie demanded when Rachel rang her the next day.

The truth was Rachel hadn't immediately answered. She had looked at Geoffrey, his round face shiny under the restaurant lights, his shirt straining at the belly (he'd put on weight lately). Did she love him? She certainly thought she did. She enjoyed the time they spent together and while things hadn't improved for her in the bedroom, she decided it was okay, that if everything else in their relationship was good, she couldn't complain, could she? And besides, she was feeling positive for the future; they had vaguely talked about having children and she wasn't getting any younger.

'I said yes, of course I said yes!' she exclaimed happily.

Rosie didn't like Geoffrey. Rachel's mother didn't like Geoffrey. The two people she trusted most in the world didn't like the man she wanted to spend her life with.

Rosie had been cautious from the beginning.

'It's all so fast,' she'd say to Rachel. 'Are you sure?' she asked a dozen times.

They'd argued several times, always after Rachel had told her about something Geoffrey had done like missing a dinner because he was out with the boys, or a comment he'd made about Rachel's mother ('she doesn't smile much does she?'). Their arguments always ending with Rachel defending him, 'You don't know him as I do,' before angrily ending the conversation.

The discord meant Rachel couldn't share her concern about what was happening (or not happening) in the bedroom. It was the first time in their long friendship she'd been unable to confide in her.

Later she asked Rosie what she had seen in Geoffrey that Rachel failed to.

Rosie thought long and hard before answering. 'You thought you were in love, Rachel. You saw what you wanted to see but he never looked at you the way you looked at him.'

Rachel loved Geoffrey's little two-bedroom house. It had a tiny garden and a small sun-drenched patio.

'We can have barbecues, invite the neighbours,' she said happily.

'We don't want to be doing that, I don't want to share you with anyone,' he said winking at her as he opened a beer, slurping it as it gushed out of the can. She didn't question him, taking what he said at face value.

She regularly saw her mother and Rosie but by some unspoken agreement Geoffrey wasn't included, and while it saddened her they couldn't all get along, she accepted it was the only chink in the armour of what she now viewed as her near-perfect life.

For the first six months, she was blissfully happy. Her heart leapt with happiness every morning when she saw their two toothbrushes together. She set about adding feminine touches, new curtains, a bright doona cover for their bed. She kept the house spotlessly clean, spent hours in the garden tending to the flowerbeds, and cooking elaborate meals for the two of them.

When the alarm bells began to ring, Rachel either didn't hear them or chose to ignore them — something she later spent many hours thinking about.

Chapter Nine

One night Geoffrey came in from work and headed straight to the kitchen.

'Where's my dinner?' he said, eyebrows raised.

'Oh, sorry, I had a headache most of the day. I had a nap this afternoon and I've only just got up,' said Rachel wearily rubbing her forehead.

He looked at her with something close to disgust. She was wearing her old dressing gown; her hair was oily and lank, her face devoid of make-up.

'You and your headaches.' He looked at her with hard eyes, grabbed a beer and switched on the television.

Rachel massaged her head trying to alleviate the pain. It was not the first time she felt the need to apologise to him; to her growing discomfit it was becoming a regular occurrence.

Geoffrey convinced her to give up work soon after she had moved in.

'Darling, you don't need to work. I earn enough for us both,' Geoffrey said checking his emails.

Truth be told, Rachel didn't take much convincing, after all, it wasn't like she had a high-powered career she had devoted years to establishing.

'And it's not as if it was much of a job,' Geoffrey said.

Rachel would never forget the night Geoffrey first hurt her.

'What are you wearing?' he said, looking at her as he dropped his car keys on the side table one evening.

'What do you mean?'

She was wearing an old pair of tracksuit pants, with a long-sleeved denim shirt that had seen better days. Her hair was in a messy ponytail, and she hadn't bothered with make-up given she'd been at home all day and had spent a lot of it gardening.

'I've had a long day, I'm exhausted — the least you could do is look presentable when I come home,' he said. His eyes were dark.

'I spent most of the day getting rid of the weeds, darling. I'm not going to dress up for that am I?' She came forward to kiss him, smiling, still unaware what she was walking into.

Geoffrey grabbed her arm tight and twisted it, his eyes menacing as they bore into hers.

'You look disgusting. At least try to make an effort,' he said sneeringly before walking away.

She rubbed at her arm, a nasty bruise already forming, in shock at what just happened.

Later he apologised. He had a new boss who was breathing down his neck, questioning every decision he made.

'I'm just a bit stressed. I love you, and you're so pretty, I just like to see you looking your best. It makes me happy to see you looking nice when I come home. Try to do that for me won't you?'

She had a restless night, questioning herself. Her rational mind knew she hadn't done anything wrong. But she must have, she reasoned, otherwise, why would he react in such a way?

From that day she learnt to be careful about her appearance. No matter what she was doing or what she was wearing, an hour before she knew he was due to come home, she would do her make-up and make sure she was wearing something she knew he would approve of.

She didn't dare tell Rosie. It continued to distress her that she could no longer share everything with her best friend.

Rachel sighed as she flushed the toilet and washed her hands. Her period had arrived. They had been trying for a baby for a while. Sex had not improved for her but she viewed it as a means to an end. If only she could get pregnant she thought, close to tears again.

She made a cup of camomile tea and pushed a comforting hot water bottle onto her cramping stomach.

Geoffrey wasn't going to be happy, she thought.

'You need to go back to the doctor, there must be something wrong,' he said to her the month before.

She had already been back to see her doctor twice. Her doctor, a kindly man in his fifties, had been patient with her, advising her to track her cycle to know when she was ovulating, prescribing her folic supplements, calcium and vitamin B 6. Most of all, he told her to relax, let nature take its course, that stressing unduly was not going to help. 'You're in perfect health,' he said, smiling at her.

'There's nothing wrong, I told you what the doctor said. Perhaps...' she replied defensively.

'What?'

'Well, do you think you should see the doctor?' she ventured.

'Don't be stupid, Rachel, there's nothing wrong with me,' he said storming out.

'Rachel, hi,'

'Rosie, how are you?'

'Umm, I'm okay, but I was worried when I hadn't heard from you. I wanted to check in.'

Rachel was confused. What was she talking about?

'I called last week. Geoffrey answered, and I asked him to give you a message to call me. Did you not get the message?'

Rachel was silent and angry for a moment.

'Rosie, I'm so sorry. I did get the message, but I've been so busy. Sorry, time got away,' her voice trailed off.

She could tell Rosie knew she was lying.

'I spoke to Rosie today,' she said over dinner that night.

'Oh yeah,' grunted Geoffrey one eye on the television.

'She said she gave you a message last week, for me to call her.'

'Yeah, so what's the problem?'

'You didn't give me the message. She rang today because she hadn't heard from me.'

'Jeez, what is this? Are you two joined at the hip or something? And I did give you the message.'

'Geoffrey, you didn't, I would have remembered,' said Rachel, looking him in the eye. He got up from the table, plate in one hand. He walked past Rachel, ruffled her hair, and said, 'Of course I did. We all forget things. Don't worry about it.'

On the weekends when the sun was shining and they were pottering in the garden or out at a pub lunch, or when they went for a walk or took in a movie and Geoffrey held her hand, she'd feel happy and forget about things that had happened in the week and believe again they could make their relationship work.

Money was becoming a problem. They had enough money; she just didn't like asking for it.

'I think I want to go back to work,' she said one night when they were sitting on the patio. The air was warm, and she could hear kids playing in the street. Not for the first time she wished he was more willing to make friends or entertain. She'd smiled at the woman next door a few times and would have loved to engage in a conversation. But that would lead to all sorts of awkwardness when invitations were extended, and the mere thought of negotiating with him just so she could have a cup of tea with a neighbour exhausted her.

'Why?' said Geoffrey.

'Well, it would be nice if I was earning again, you know, contributing too.'

'Don't I provide for you?'

'Oh, of course you do, I just thought it would help, you know...'

'Look, the doctor said you should avoid stress if you want to get pregnant, and that's what we want, isn't it?'

She nodded.

'So, see, I don't think it's a good idea, and it's tough out there. Remember you don't have a lot of skills, it might be hard for you to get another job. Do you want another wine?'

Christmas was soon upon them.

'Let's do some Christmas shopping tonight,' she asked him one morning.

'Can't, drinks with some suppliers,' he grimaced as if it was imposition even though she knew he enjoyed it — the drinks, the banter. He'd been out almost every night.

She absent-mindedly pulled at a thread on the bedroom throw. 'Are partners invited to the office Christmas party?'

'Nope, sorry love, have to go,' he said, leaving for work.

'I'm sure you could go if you wanted to, given you used to work there,' said Rosie when they spoke later.

'No, it's no partners, it's due to cost or something,' Rachel replied. 'Anyway, what are your plans for Christmas?'

Rachel could hear the kids bickering in the background; Beth (Rachel's godchild) who was six going on sixteen, and Tom, who was three and luckily didn't seem to mind being bossed about by his older sister.

Despite any bad blood between Geoffrey and Rosie, Rachel spoke to her friend nearly every week.

'Nice change of subject,' said Rosie drily.

Rosie knew Rachel didn't tell her everything. And while Rosie respected that some things between a couple couldn't and shouldn't be shared, she suspected Rachel was not as happy as she made out to be.

'Hang on a minute,' said Rosie. 'Beth, stop that right now. Yes, now. Good girl, now sit quietly.'

Rachel was laughing, 'What was she doing this time?'

'She was rubbing vegemite all over Tom's face, and bless him, he doesn't even mind, just sits there looking adoringly at her.'

They both chuckled.

'I'm sorry Rachel,' said Rosie quietly.

'Don't be. We're still trying. It will happen, I know it,' she said, sounding more positive than she felt.

She was becoming less optimistic by the day. They were still having sex regularly, but Geoffrey acted like she wasn't even there. If he'd been out after work, he'd come home smelling of beer, and even if she was sleeping, he'd paw at her and be on top of her before she could protest. She'd tried to tell him it hurt and that she wasn't ready, but he never listened, and after a while, it was easier to silently give in.

She still had romantic notions about how this relationship could turn out. In her mind, all she needed to do was try harder.

They spent Christmas with Geoffrey's sister, Michaela, and her husband, Vince. Michaela was a senior manager at a bank, and Vince worked in real estate. They lived in a big house in Sydney's eastern suburbs. They had two teenagers who steadfastly ignored them, and spent the day playing video games.

Michaela and Geoffrey shared the same nose and eye shape. Apart from that, they couldn't look more different. Geoffrey wore whatever he grabbed out of the wardrobe: standard t-shirts, or shirts, with (on this occasion) ill-fitting jeans. His sister, however, was stylish in head-to-toe cream linen, expensive jewellery her only adornment. Vince was similarly attired complete with a liberal dabbing of expensive aftershave.

She liked Vince. He was a born salesperson with a gift of the gab, but he was a good host ready with a joke, topping up her glass and involving her in the conversation.

It was obvious Geoffrey was jealous of what his sister had achieved. Rachel caught him — his face like thunder — studying the new barbecue, the large television, the two BMWs, mentally adding up what everything must have cost.

The siblings were clearly not close as this was the first time Rachel had met Michaela and Vince. They usually only saw each other at Christmas, maintaining some sort of forced familial connection now that their parents were dead.

Lunch was a huge seafood platter complete with oysters, prawns, calamari, and salmon. Accompanied by fresh sourdough bread and three beautiful summer salads. Champagne and a choice of wines were offered.

'Gosh, how did you find the time to do this?' said Rachel to Michaela. She knew they had been at Vince's parents most of the morning.

Michaela laughed at her naivety. 'I didn't, we paid someone to do it,' she said, enjoying the look on her brother's face.

Even with the free-flowing alcohol, the conversation was stilted and forced. They all played their parts: Michaela took every opportunity to flaunt their wealth and status; Geoffrey threw barbs at his sister or muttered under his breath, and Vince tried to keep the peace by steering the conversation to calmer topics when he sensed a storm brewing. Rachel said little, both fascinated and disturbed by the wealth on display and embarrassed by her boyfriend and his sister's behaviour.

Chapter Ten

After the mostly silent drive home, Geoffrey immediately opened a beer, went straight outside and sat on the patio staring into the distance. An hour later, Rachel joined him, carrying two coffees.

She sat down and took a sip of her coffee.

'Did you get on when you were kids?' she asked, more to fill the silence than genuinely wanting to know.

Geoffrey turned slowly and looked at her.

'You were impressed, were you?'

'What? Well sort of, I...I...mean the house and everything, you have to admit...' said Rachel starting to stutter nervously under his gaze.

'If you liked it so much, why don't you fuck off and live there?' He got up and went inside for another beer.

'I'm sorry,' he said a few hours later.

Rachel had been sitting inside watching carols on the television, reminiscing about Christmases past. Her mother made every Christmas special, even if they didn't have much — a small tree, a stocking, milk left out for Santa. On Christmas Day, they'd eat ham and pull crackers and watch the carols or a movie together.

She said nothing.

'I'd had too much to drink. I can't give you what she has. I'm sorry that I can't but that's the way it is.'

'I don't want those things, I never have. I love you,' she said. Maybe things were going to get better, she thought, maybe he'd just been worried about providing for her. Men were funny like that. It was true, she didn't want expensive jewellery or a new car, she just wanted them to be happy. Maybe it was a good thing that today had happened, perhaps it had cleared the air.

'Perhaps we could have an early night?' she said winding her arm around his neck and stroking his cheek, surprised at her boldness.

Geoffrey lifted her arm away. 'If you don't mind, I think I'll go for a walk. I need to clear my head, and I ate too much today!'

He glanced down and prodded at Rachel's bloated stomach. 'I think you did too fatty, how much pavlova did you eat?'

Stung by the rejection and hurtful words, she tearfully changed into her pyjamas and went to bed alone.

Merry Bloody Christmas.

'What did Geoffrey get you for Christmas?' asked Rosie the next day.

'Umm, a SodaStream,' replied Rachel down the phone.

Rosie snorted. 'I don't think Bruce would dare get me a kitchen appliance for Christmas, I think he values his life too much.'

Rachel was immediately defensive. 'Well, he likes it, I mean, we both do. I think it's a great present,' she said.

'Sorry Rachel, I didn't mean to offend. As long as you're happy.'

She said nothing.

Geoffrey was angry. She'd just got her period. Again.

Rachel thought he was becoming obsessed with getting her pregnant.

'We can keep trying, can't we? It will happen I'm sure of it,' said Rachel trying to convince herself as much as him.

He stormed out, said he was going to the pub.

'What does your doctor say?' asked Rosie when they spoke next.

'He said everything was fine, that medically nothing is stopping me from falling pregnant. He just says we need to relax and keep trying.'

'Well, he's right. How's Geoffrey taking it?'

Rachel was silent. 'Well, he's disappointed of course. He would do anything for us to become parents,' she said unconvincingly.

'Except get tested himself,' said Rosie disparagingly. Rachel had forgotten she had told her that.

Again Rachel felt unable to talk to Rosie. She was tired; tired of keeping Geoffrey happy, tired of being disappointed about not being able to fall pregnant; and tired of trying to convince Rosie that everything truly was fine.

'What shall we do on the weekend?' Rachel asked Geoffrey one Friday morning when they were having breakfast. He usually had to work on Saturday mornings but was having a rare morning off and she knew he was looking forward to it.

'Oh, I forgot to tell you, I'm playing golf on Saturday. I haven't been to the club for a while so I'm catching up with a few blokes I used to play with. It will be good to be back out there,' he said, getting up to put his cereal bowl in the sink and doing a mock golf swing as he walked back out of the kitchen.

'Well maybe I could meet you after, come to the club,' said Rachel. 'I've never been there and it would be nice to meet more of your friends.'

'Maybe another time,' said Geoffrey grabbing his keys. 'Is that the time? I have to go, see you tonight.'

She went into the kitchen to wash the breakfast dishes. 'What's the point?' she muttered to herself.

Days turned into weeks, weeks into months. Their relationship became predictable in the most unpredictable ways. For a while they'd be fine, then she'd do or say something that would irritate Geoffrey, or he'd be in a bad mood and take it out on her. He'd call her names, told her she was ugly, that she was lazy. Then he'd apologise, blame it on work stress.

Every month her period appeared like clockwork; he'd look at her with a mixture of pity, blame and disgust. If she tried to broach the subject of going back to work, the response was the same — she was never going to get pregnant if she had the added stress of holding down a job, even if she could get a job, which he seriously doubted; and besides didn't he provide for her? Didn't he give her everything she wanted?

Later, she wondered why she didn't just leave. Too weak was her first thought, berating herself. But over time and talking it over with Rosie she realised why.

'I always hoped things would improve. Maybe deep down I realised Geoffrey wasn't the right man for me, but I just kept hoping things would get better.'

She was also embarrassed to admit that she didn't want to leave her financial stability. Was there something wrong with wanting to be financially secure? She didn't want to leave the comfortable little house and see if she could make it on her own, no matter how unhappy she became with his erratic moods. She was convinced they could make it work, that she had provoked him in some way, and that if she could only make him happy, they could have a future together.

So, she'd stayed.

She was pregnant!

She stared at the home pregnancy test kit in her hands (the second she'd done that morning), sitting on the toilet seat as she waited, trying to calm her excitement — she was going to be a mum! She was sure she looked maniacal, smiling like an idiot. Time was up. She looked. She punched the air, yes! Two tests couldn't be wrong.

Washing her hands, she looked in the mirror, turning sideways, but of course, there was no bump, nothing to look at yet. Yet still she cradled her stomach, grinning.

Walking into the kitchen she picked up her phone to ring Geoffrey but hesitated. He hated it when she rang him at work but surely, he'd want to hear from her straight away? Maybe she'd wait until he got home. But, no, he'd definitely want her to ring him. It wasn't every day you found out you were going to be a father.

Then she remembered the last time she'd called him at work. She'd copped it from him that night, yelling at her that she had no idea what real life was like if she thought it was okay to interrupt him as she had. No, she'd wait until he was home. At the back of her mind, she was thinking that surely something was wrong with their relationship if she couldn't even be sure of the best way to tell the father of her child that in nine months they were going to be parents. She pushed the uncomfortable thoughts from her mind; today was a happy day. Her mind made up, she decided to ring Rosie, then her mother.

Rosie was ecstatic for her! Laughing and crying together, Rachel thought she'd done the right thing ringing her first. Being a mum, she knew exactly what she was feeling. Rosie said she must go and see her doctor as soon as possible, get it all confirmed.

'Way ahead of you, I've got an appointment tomorrow,' said Rachel. When she'd been debating who to ring first, she'd suddenly realised seeing her doctor was just as important.

'What did Geoffrey say?' asked Rosie. 'He must be so happy!'

Rachel was silent for a moment. She didn't want to tell Rosie that she was too scared to ring him at work, that she thought it was better to wait until he was home.

'He's so happy and promised to wait on me hand and foot,' lied Rachel.

'And so he should — wait until you get cravings.' Rosie had had the most peculiar cravings — ice cream and olives; cheese with tomato sauce — and Bruce had never once faltered as he tended to every one of her demands. Rachel couldn't see Geoffrey adopting the same role.

Her mother's reaction had been equally as warm but hesitant.

'Does that mean you're going to get married?' she asked.

Rachel readied herself for the evening. She made a roast with baked potatoes, one of Geoffrey's favourite meals. She made sure there was beer in the fridge and put on a dress she knew he liked.

When Geoffrey came home, she was outside reading on the patio.

'Hello, did you have a good day?' she asked putting her book down.

'Not too bad.'

'It's nice out here this evening. Sit down and relax, I'll get you a beer,' she said getting up, glad he seemed in a good mood.

'Not having one?' he said when she returned.

She looked at him, a smile forming on her lips. 'No, not tonight,' she said. She took a step closer to him, so she was standing right in front of him.

'You okay?' he asked.

Rachel took his hands in hers, then slowly moved them so they were touching her stomach. 'I'm pregnant,' she said softly.

Geoffrey looked at her in amazement, as if he couldn't believe it. He grinned and hugged her tight. 'You're sure?'

'Well, I did two tests, and I'm going to see the doctor tomorrow, but yes, I'm sure. I feel it you know. I feel different.'

He twirled her around as she laughed. The night was perfect. He was attentive, loving. Just like the early days she thought. They went to bed early, with her curled up against him.

'You can ring Rosie and your mum tomorrow,' said Geoffrey.

The next couple of weeks were wonderful. When Geoffrey was home, he tended to her every need, even doing the laundry and ironing which he had previously derided as 'women's work.' She made plans for the nursery, looked at baby clothes and maternity dresses, humming as she went about her day.

When she was nineteen weeks pregnant her life changed.

Chapter Eleven

Geoffrey came home after work one day and found Rachel surrounded by baby clothes.

'Where did these come from?' he said picking up a yellow onesie.

'Rosie.' She held up a tiny orange singlet. 'Have you ever seen anything so cute? These are all old things of Beth and Tom's and even though we don't know what we're having yet, a lot of them are neutral colours.'

'We don't need hand-me-downs,' said Geoffrey his mouth set in a grim line.

Rachel picked up a small sun hat again not seeing what she was walking into.

'Oh, they're just from Rosie, and she doesn't need them anymore.' She was about to tell him that Rosie had virtually frogmarched Bruce down to the surgery to get a vasectomy when she looked up and saw Geoffrey's face.

'You'll return them tomorrow,' he said stiffly.

'Geoffrey, honestly, Rosie knows we can afford our own things, she's just being helpful, honestly,' she said.

'Tomorrow, you'll pack this shit up and send it back to Saint Rosie. I don't want her and her dumb witted husband thinking I can't afford to clothe my own son.' Geoffrey's face was close to her, and she could feel spittle on her face as she shrunk back into the couch.

They spent the night in silence. As she was getting ready for bed, something was niggling at the back of her mind, but she couldn't grasp it. In the middle of the night, she awoke with a start.

'Son,' she thought. Geoffrey had said 'son' even though they didn't know what they were having. She shivered in the dark before falling into a fitful sleep, a protective hand on her bump. How would he react if they had a little girl?

A few days later she was pottering in the garden one afternoon when she heard a voice call out 'hello.' Rachel looked up and saw the woman next door, head peering over the fence.

'I saw you out in the garden and thought I'd say hi. Gorgeous day, isn't it?' the woman said. Rachel guessed she was in her late twenties, short blonde hair, a liberal smattering of freckles on her face.

'It sure is.'

'I was just going to put the kettle on,' said the woman who was called Kayleigh. 'Do you want to come over?'

Rachel hesitated. She could hardly tell the woman her partner didn't want her socialising with her. She glanced at her watch. Geoffrey wouldn't be home for hours, what harm could it do?

'I'd love that,' she said. 'I'll just wash my hands and be round in a minute.'

Half an hour later she and Kayleigh were chatting as if they had known each other for months not minutes.

'Gosh, how on earth do you manage?' asked Rachel after learning that Kayleigh and her husband Brett had four-year-old-twins.

Kayleigh laughed. 'Well, half the time we don't. We just muddle through together. One thing you learn about becoming a mum is that you can't stress if things aren't perfect. Who cares if the house is a bit messy?' she said waving her arm around. 'As long as the kids are happy and healthy, and Brett and I are good, isn't that all that matters?'

Rachel agreed although part of her was wondering how Geoffrey, who was very set in his ways would deal with that.

Kayleigh was delighted to learn Rachel was pregnant and promised to lend her what she said was the ONLY baby book she would ever need.

Two cups of tea and three Tim Tams later, Rachel went back home, making a date with Kayleigh for later in the week to go to the park with her and the twins. Maybe once Geoffrey got to know them, he'd warm to the idea of socialising occasionally, she thought.

The next morning, she was in the shower when she heard the front doorbell ring. Geoffrey hadn't left for work yet, so she assumed he'd get it. She assumed right as she soon heard the murmur of conversation. She idly wondered who it could be at this early hour?

She sensed a shift in the atmosphere as soon as she walked into the kitchen. Geoffrey was standing at the sink looking out the window, his neck muscles taut. A book she hadn't seen before was lying on the table. She looked at the cover, *You and Baby: Everything You Need to Know.*

Geoffrey slowly turned around. He didn't say anything, just stared at her.

'Your friend came over this morning,' he said eventually, enunciating the word *friend* slowly.

Rachel didn't say anything. She suddenly felt scared, fearful; she was familiar with his moods, but this felt different.

'Don't you have anything to say?' Geoffrey said slowly drawing the words out as he moved towards her.

'Geoffrey, she's really nice, we just had a chat, and she said she'd lend me—'

'Shut up!' shouted Geoffrey. 'I'm sick and tired of you going behind my back; disobeying me.'

Pressed up against the island bench, the solid granite digging painfully into her lower back she began to whimper. 'Move Geoffrey, please, you're hurting me.'

Geoffrey pinned her arms behind her and pushed hard up against her again. She started to sob. It made no difference; his mouth was curled into an ugly, perverse smile. He was enjoying watching her writhe in pain and distress.

Suddenly he let her go and roughly pushed her aside. She heard the slam of the front door and the car starting. She collapsed to the floor, letting out a deep breath she didn't realise she'd been holding.

She must have sat there for a while. As she gingerly lifted herself off the floor, she felt something warm gush down her legs. Blood.

Chapter Twelve

'He was a monster,' Rosie said quietly bringing her back to the present day.

'That could have been me.'

'Do you want me to come to Sydney?'

'No, no Rosie, I'll be okay.'

'I think you should go to the police.'

'Why? What would I need to do that for?' Rachel was confused.

'I don't know really, but I just feel you could tell them about his behaviour, so they have the full picture of what that bastard was like,' she said.

They talked for a while, each reluctant to hang up. Eventually they did, Rachel promising she would ring her again in the morning.

She still hadn't moved by the time Leah got home later that day. Leah took one look at her friend's drawn face and knew something had happened.

Haltingly Rachel filled her in. That afternoon, the tension over the five hundred dollars dwindled as Leah never left her side, talking when she wanted to, sitting quietly at other times.

Later that evening they sat having yet another cup of tea together. Rachel hadn't been able to keep any food down, but the tea was calming.

'How are you feeling?' asked Leah.

Rachel paused before she answered. 'Numb, shocked, tired. Guilty, lucky.'

She looked at Leah. 'Is it wrong that I feel lucky?'

She shook her head. 'No. It just means you're human.'

Rachel looked at Leah gratefully; she was glad she wasn't alone.

Leah agreed with Rosie's suggestion that Rachel visit the police. 'I'm in no hurry to see the inside of a police station again, but I'll go with you,' she said reluctantly.

Rosie was right, the police were interested. She spoke to a very kind and understanding female detective, who was accompanied by a policeman who looked much too young to be dealing with such horrible issues.

She calmly answered their questions, describing how controlling Geoffrey had been, his erratic behaviour, the bullying, the silent treatment. How one minute he could be kind, the next malicious.

When she was leaving, the female detective placed a gentle hand on Rachel's shoulder.

'Are you okay?' she asked.

'I don't know, I feel numb really,' said Rachel. 'The woman...?'

'I can't say too much about the case, but it's believed they had been together for a few years,' the detective said.

Rachel looked like she wanted to ask something but didn't know how to. Or perhaps didn't want to ask for fear of what the answer would reveal.

'When we were together, well I told you what he was like, but to kill someone... I mean, how? Geoffrey wasn't like that, well maybe he was. I don't— '

The detective thought for a moment before answering.

'His behaviour escalated over the years. From what you say he was trying to control you. There's a lot we know about domestic violence but a lot we don't. You've been very brave in coming forward and telling us your story. It helps, believe me. It all helps.'

Rachel smiled weakly, accepting a pamphlet for a counselling service.

Later she learnt the woman had taken out an AVO against Geoffrey as a last resort, that previously she had confided in her friends about his behaviour but was convinced he would change — that things would get better.

As she walked home from the police station with Leah, memories from the day she had lost her baby came flooding back. She had yelled out, first in pain and shock, and then louder as she realised she needed help. Luckily Kayleigh was in her backyard and came running and called an ambulance. Kayleigh assumed Rachel had slipped in the kitchen and she didn't correct her. Even in her physical distress, she knew she'd never see her neighbour again.

At the hospital nurses fired questions at her. She heard whispered voices. But she'd already known. She knew as soon as she had collapsed in the kitchen. Her baby was gone.

They'd gently told her it was a girl. No one questioned her about the line of colourful bruises on her lower back.

She asked a nurse to call her mother who immediately rushed to the hospital. Rachel and her mother clutched each other until she was allowed to go home. Her mother tucked her up in her old bed; a much-loved teddy bear from her childhood next to her.

The hospital had given Rachel something to help her sleep. It didn't seem to do much and afterwards, she was glad — the memory of her mother sitting by her bed all night was a precious one.

Weak and fragile, and scared to face him, she sent Geoffrey a text telling him she had miscarried. Two days later her phone beeped.

I want you out of the house

After she miscarried, Rosie had been on the phone with her constantly.

'I don't know what I'm feeling — sad, angry, scared. I lost a baby but...'

'You're thinking about how it would have been if your daughter had survived, growing up with him as her father?' said Rosie seeming to read her mind as usual.

It had been Rosie who slowly coaxed her into calling the baby 'her daughter'.

'Yes. Is that wrong?'

'No,' said Rosie firmly. 'It shows what a good mother you would have been and that you will be one day.'

If she saw a baby, she would flinch, turn her eyes away quickly. Walking past children's clothing stores or day-care centres she would avert her eyes, stuffing her hands in her pockets as she hurried past. She hadn't realised there were so many babies. They were everywhere.

'Why me, Rosie, why did he pick me?'

'He was a bully,' she said, 'None of this was your fault.'

Rachel didn't believe her; she was haunted by memories. Was it because she had been so easily swayed by his sweet talk when he was a store manager? Did he realise his phone calls were the highlight of her lonely weeks? Or was it her naivety and lack of self-confidence that made her an easy target for a bully like him? Was it about power, ego, satisfying a desire to control her, proving how simple it was?

None of the answers satisfied her or silenced the voice in her head that kept saying, 'you let this happen.'

'On the one hand, I feel so old and tired and washed up but I'm also starting from scratch,' she'd tried to explain to Rosie. Her ordeal weighed heavily on her; she was anxious all the time. After the miscarriage she lived with her mother, had little money, had to re-enter the workforce, and what little job skills she did have were average at best.

Rachel and Leah had promised Amira they would take her to the park one day and apparently today was the day. She felt emotionally exhausted and completely wrung out since fainting at the library, and it was the last thing she felt like doing as much as she loved spending time with Amira. She suspected Leah and Rima had hatched the plan, so after she and Leah returned from an early morning cleaning shift they set off.

Amira walked between them, holding their hands. The park was crowded; they sat on a bench and observed the scene in front of them. Parents clutched takeaway coffees. Kids of all ages were running around, fearlessly scampering up the climbing frame, tumbling down slides, or sitting in the sandpit. Next to the playground, kids were practising on their tricycles under the watchful eye of parents, the cry of 'pedal!' piercing through the air.

Amira sat between them, suddenly shy.

'Do you want to go and play?' said Rachel, pointing in front of her.

'Looks like fun,' Leah added.

Amira shook her head and nestled into them. Rachel and Leah exchanged a look over her head.

After a few minutes, Leah stood up. 'Well, I'm ready to play,' she announced rolling up her sleeves.

'You,' giggled Amira. 'You're too old!'

'Old? Who are you calling old?' Leah roared in a mock scary voice picking up Amira and tickling her.

Amira giggled even louder. 'Shoulders,' she demanded. Leah put her on her shoulders and walked to the edge of the play area before carefully placing a still giggling Amira on the ground. Amira immediately ran off and happily started climbing across one of the little bridges.

'Nicely done,' said Rachel, smiling.

Rachel watched the two of them. Leah didn't once take her eyes off Amira, watching her carefully. Today, Leah's hair was orange. She was dressed in an old Def Leppard t-shirt and worn-out black tracksuit pants, a shabby pink scarf wrapped around her neck. She was giggling at something Amira said, her wide mouth revealing her two missing teeth.

Rachel noticed a few of the mothers staring at Leah, and a couple of them even moved away, seemingly put off by the brow-ringed-orange-haired woman who was making funny cross-eyed faces at a near hysterical Amira.

Rachel was annoyed. Despite their differences and the incident over the money, she was fiercely protective of Leah; she stepped off the bench and took a seat beside her friend, earning more pointed looks from the self-satisfied looking mothers near them.

Rachel whispered something to Leah.

Leah turned and looked at the women who quickly turned the other way. 'Any of you a dentist?' yelled Leah baring her toothless smile.

The women looked embarrassed, as Leah and Rachel burst into laughter. Her friends had been right, the visit to the park had been just what she needed.

For weeks after, Rachel would wake up and, after a few moments of blissful peace, would recall the news about Geoffrey, and her mind would spiral, thoughts flying in all directions. It was the last thing she thought about before going to bed and it occupied her mind throughout the day. It was no surprise she was exhausted most of the time.

Even Amira seemed to sense something. When Rachel was minding her, instead of boisterously playing and shouting for attention she would sometimes snuggle up to Rachel, watching TV quietly, or listening to her reading, her little hand tucked into hers.

She became obsessed with the dead woman. Had she loved Geoffrey? Had she spent awful Christmases with his sister? What were her last thoughts before she was stabbed to death?

She lived with a suffocating sense of guilt for being alive. And she'd wake up in the middle of the night, struggling to breathe. He could have killed her.

It could have been me on the front page of the newspaper.

She continued with the casual cleaning work. It exhausted her, numbed her. She was eventually able to sleep for at least a few hours each night. Her appetite grew stronger.

She didn't know exactly when she decided that she wanted to speak to Geoffrey's sister Michaela. It wasn't like she thought Michaela would be able to answer any of the questions she had.

Perhaps she just wanted to speak to someone who knew Geoffrey, someone who may be feeling like she was.

She googled Michaela and saw that she and her husband had started up some sort of business consultancy. She found the website and Michaela's mobile number. She hesitated but knew if she didn't ring now, she'd chicken out.

Even after such a long time, Rachel immediately recognised the clipped polished voice that answered the phone.

At first, Rachel froze, then found her voice. 'Michaela, you might not remember me, but I...'

'Yes?' said Michaela impatiently.

'My name's Rachel Farrowsworth, I met you a few times when I lived with Geoffrey.' She heard the sharp intake of breath from the other woman.

'Yes, I remember you,' said Michaela. 'Sorry to be blunt but what do you want?'

Rude as ever thought Rachel.

She cleared her throat. 'Obviously, I know about what happened, and I...' Rachel's voice trailed.

'What?'

'I was shocked by what happened, and I'm struggling to get past it if I'm honest, I mean that poor woman,' said Rachel. 'Look,' she continued. 'Could we meet perhaps, for a coffee or something? I just want to talk to you.'

'I don't honestly know what the point of that—'

'Do you feel guilty?' Rachel interrupted Michaela. 'I know I do. Guilty that I'm alive and that poor woman isn't and guilty that maybe I could have done something to prevent him going on to do this.' Feeling emboldened, she continued, 'And I bet you do too.'

This time Michaela's tone was slightly softer. 'We could meet in the city near my office,' she said.

A few days later Rachel arrived at the café in the city at the agreed time. Even though it had been years since they had seen each other, Rachel would have recognised Michaela anywhere. She was still a stylish woman, clad in stylish black silk flowing pants with a soft pink shirt, expensive silver jewellery, a slash of red lipstick on her perfectly made-up face.

Rachel made her way over to the table. 'Hi Michaela.'

Up close she could see that Michaela may have had a helping hand with her face. Wait till I tell Rosie, she thought.

For a few moments, they busied themselves with ordering coffees.

'Thanks for meeting me,' said Rachel.

They said nothing for a while.

'You must have been shocked when you heard about it,' said Michaela.

Rachel described how she had been in the library when she'd seen the article, how she collapsed, and had struggled since then. She told Michaela she had been to the police.

Michaela raised her eyebrows at this. 'What did you tell them?'

'I just told them about the relationship, what went on, his behaviour and how it ended.'

'What do you mean how it ended? You walked out on him. He told us you went back to an old boyfriend,' said Michaela.

Rachel looked at her incredulously. She told her about the hurt Geoffrey had inflicted on her, and about the miscarriage.

'We had no idea about that, I'm sorry, Rachel,' Michaela looked at her with genuine sympathy.

'I keep asking myself whether I could have done anything to prevent it,' said Rachel.

Their coffees arrived and it was a while before Michaela spoke. 'We weren't close. Geoffrey was a bully, even as a child. He was also a very jealous person. He played with people, manipulated them, he knew how to get what he wanted. But he wasn't smart. He got kicked out of university for cheating, did he tell you that?'

Rachel shook her head.

'He couldn't live with the fact that Vince and I had what we had or indeed anyone else. He hated successful people.'

Rachel remembered the way he had looked at Michaela's house, at the BMWs.

'He didn't respect or understand, or maybe he chose not to understand, to see all the hard work, the hours of study, the sacrifice. That jealousy turned ugly. Bullying was the only way he knew how to deal with it.'

'Did you meet...Sharna?'

'Only once, and I liked her. She was a real estate agent, a real go-getter.'

Not like me, Rachel thought.

As if sensing what Rachel was thinking Michaela said, 'I remember that Christmas lunch, god he was awful that day. Afterwards, I said to Vince that I felt really bad about you.'

Rachel must have looked surprised.

'You were easy to talk to, you were good company, and Geoffrey was just, ugh, that day,' said Michaela.

'Look, Rachel, I can't help you in not feeling guilty. I've been going to counselling about this,' she paused. 'Vince and I noticed his anger had definitely been increasing over the years, but we were never close, we hardly saw him. We had no idea it would escalate to something like this,' she said almost defensively. 'You can't feel guilty, you can't blame yourself. Besides the fact you couldn't have done anything about it, I can tell you already suffered enough at his hands.'

They parted not long after, each feeling a little better perhaps, but also relieved knowing they would never have to see each other again.

Chapter Thirteen

'I got a job! I got a job!' Lin was justifiably overjoyed.

'Lin, that's fantastic,' Rachel exclaimed, high fiving her.

Lin had gotten a job as an assistant accountant ('I should be the accountant, and I'm reporting to someone half my age, but it's a job,' Lin had told her in a voice that meant it was safer not to argue) and was happily sharing her news.

There was more good news too. Leah had secured work as a permanent cleaner, with regular shifts. She'd completed cleaning courses through NSW JobTrainer as part of the job, and she'd got good references.

To celebrate their change in fortune, Lin invited her, Leah, and Rima to her house for lunch where she was going to cook a Malaysian feast. Everyone was excited. Rachel hadn't looked forward to anything in such a long time. Rima was looking forward to eating Malaysian food which she'd never tried (although Rachel wasn't sure how Rima would cope sitting still while someone waited on her!).

Lunch was a great success.

Lin's son and daughter-in-law greeted everyone when they arrived, sorted out the drinks for them, and then departed wishing them a happy lunch, her son giving his mother a kiss on the cheek before cheekily adding 'don't poison your friends, Ma.'

Lin shooed him out laughing, telling him she wouldn't leave leftovers for him!

Lin had indeed put on a feast — noodles with chicken, veggies, and eggs. Vegetable curry. Satay. Flatbreads. She had been generous with the chilli. Rima was used to spicy foods, unlike Rachel and Leah who gulped what felt like litres of water.

Everyone agreed the food was delicious.

'But the company is the best,' said Rima raising her glass of orange juice.

They exchanged toasts. Rachel smiled as she looked around the table at her friends. Could four women be any more different?

Rima and Lin were wide-eyed as Leah told them about her tattoos, both looking in reverence at her forearm where *only the strong survive* could be seen inked in black.

Lin regaled them with stories about growing up in a strict Malaysian family and working hard to get her degree.

Rima explained Islam to them, answering their questions and debunking many of the misconceptions they had heard in the media.

While Leah and Rima made a start on the washing up, Lin handed Rachel a small parcel.

'What's this?' she said surprised.

'Open it,' said Lin.

She unwrapped the parcel and pulled out two beautiful silk shirts – one a golden yellow, the other a bright red with tiny gold buttons.

'Oh Lin, they're beautiful,' exclaimed Rachel. 'But I can't take these.' Even as she fingered the delicate material, she imagined wearing them, such luxurious material.

'Rachel,' Lin looked at her. 'They were sent to me from Malaysia, but they don't fit me. And I want you to have them. Time to stop hiding in your brown clothes.'

Rachel smiled. Lin had a way of being direct, but it was impossible to take offence because she was so kind.

'I know what happened, and my heart hurts for you. Wear these new shirts, you deserve colour and life,' said Lin.

Rachel hugged her friend. 'Thank you,' she whispered.

Later, armed with doggy bags, they walked back to their unit block. Or, as Leah put it, 'rolled', as they had eaten so much.

'What about my hair?' asked Rachel.

Since the last lot of job rejections, Rachel had been thinking about her appearance. She was angry she even had to think like this, but she had no choice. There could be no expensive makeovers for her but there must be something she could do, she thought desperately.

As always, she turned to her Melbourne-based-font-of-all-knowledge-and-advice.

'Maybe you should think about one of those temporary hair dyes. I know it's spending money but... I think it could help, you know hide the greys a bit,' said Rosie.

'How much do they cost?'

'You should be able to get one for about ten dollars, I think. And I think you need a new lipstick, to go with the shirts.'

Rachel had told Rosie about the shirts Lin had given her. Rosie had been delighted for her, agreeing it was time for all the brown to be given the flick.

'If you can stretch it, buy a concealer, you know just to help,' said Rosie.

'I'll need pots of the stuff to cover up this face,' she replied gloomily.

After the phone call, Rosie started doing some figures on the back of an envelope, calculating she could get the hair stuff this week, and the lipstick next week, if she could cope with instant noodles for a bit. She'd also ask Rima if she could borrow her tweezers and see if she could tidy up her eyebrows.

Human Enthusiast | Ethical Recruiter | Experience Advocate

Rachel read the title again to make sure she had it right. Yes, she had, that was indeed the title of the recruiter she was sending a job application to. This was one of those moments when she felt the world moving and changing at such a pace that not only was she struggling to keep up, but she also didn't understand it.

Sighing, Rachel pressed send and sat back in her chair as she wondered if someone called a Human Enthusiast would be enthusiastic about her job application for a warehouse assistant.

'I'm obsessed with eyebrows,' said Rosie that night.

'Eyebrows?' said Rachel bemused.

Rachel had shared the latest on her job-seeking activities. The abrupt change of subject was no surprise to her — that was Rosie all over.

'Yes, eyebrows. Growing up we did nothing with our eyebrows, maybe an eyebrow pencil that's it,' Rosie was in full flow.

'The other day in the supermarket I thought a caterpillar was crawling across this girl's face, but it wasn't, it was her eyebrows. They were so thick!'

Rachel laughed. 'You've become quite the expert.'

'It's really weird. Suddenly, I'm noticing all these young girls, and they seem to have had work done. Botox, fillers, injections. They're already so gorgeous. I don't get it,' said Rosie sounding genuinely confused.

'Rosie,' said Rachel.

'What?'

'Don't ever change.'

'What did they say?' asked Rosie.

'The first thing the manager always asks, after we interview someone is *are they sunshiny enough?*' Rachel mimicked the voice of the recruitment consultant, emphasising the word sunshiny in the same way it had been delivered to her.

She then told Rosie about the interview she had for an office assistant for a small recruitment/business networking company run by two young women.

Rachel put on the same mocking voice. 'They were sceptical as to whether I would *live and breathe the vision.*'

She paused before she continued, her voice quietened. 'Apparently, I didn't come across as motivated as some of the other candidates,' she said to her friend. 'But Rosie, that wasn't the worst.'

Even Rosie was shocked to hear that one of the women had asked her where she bought her clothes. Rachel's humiliation was so raw down the phone that Rosie knew it hadn't been meant as a compliment.

'Why can't anyone see that I'd be a dependable, steady employee? I thought these were assets but apparently not. They think I'm boring and unmotivated,' she seethed. 'I'm angry at myself too — I meekly accept all this negative feedback but what else can I do?' She was almost screeching, such was her frustration.

Rosie felt helpless. She was furious on her friend's behalf and could hear the growing sense of rage whenever they spoke.

After they'd hung up, Rachel stormed around the flat, incensed she had found herself in this situation, being rejected by people who were more than half her age.

That night Leah didn't come home.

Rachel knew she had had a cleaning shift that morning and it was unusual for her not to come straight home afterwards — she always said she couldn't wait to come home and have a shower after a shift. She went next door to Rima, thinking perhaps they'd had a play date with Amira organised, but they hadn't seen her.

She grew increasingly worried as the night wore on, her phone calls and texts to Leah going unanswered. At the back of her mind, she was thinking that recently Leah seemed preoccupied, quieter than usual. Rachel would often catch her just staring, caught up in her thoughts, but would quickly brush away Rachel's concerns. Whenever she got like that Rachel assumed she was thinking about her children.

She debated calling the police but perhaps she was being silly. Maybe Leah was just out. Rachel knew all too well how stifling the small flat could feel.

She shivered as she remembered what Leah said to her when she had been beaten up: 'Rachel, look at me, do you seriously think the police are going to care about an ex-junkie?'

Unable to sleep, Rachel set about cleaning the flat. She scrubbed the bathroom and kitchen, cleaned, mopped, and dusted. She even scrubbed at the skirting boards and windows. She was so agitated that if she could have done something there and then about the peeling paint or the carpet she would have.

As the first light of dawn crept through the curtains, Rachel's imagination was in overdrive and her empty stomach in knots.

When she answered the door to two young policewomen later that morning, she felt her knees buckle.

'Are you Rachel Farrowsworth?' asked one of the policewomen who introduced herself as Constable Peters.

'Yes,' said Rachel. 'Is it about Leah?' she whispered.

'Perhaps we could come inside?' said the other policewoman.

Leah was dead.

When Constable Peters told her Leah had been found in a park a few suburbs away, she had whispered, 'How?'

'We believe it was an overdose,' said the woman softly as she sat down next to Rachel. 'Is there anyone we can call to sit with you?' she asked.

Rima was immediately at Rachel's side, holding her hand and sobbing quietly.

'I didn't know she was using again,' Rachel said dabbing her eyes with tissues. She explained that she hadn't come home last night.

'Could you tell me a bit about her?' asked the Constable.

Rachel told her what she knew about Leah — her upbringing, her years on the street, what she knew of her children, and how she had come to live with Rachel.

'You must have been a good friend to her,' said the policewomen, telling her that they had found her name and address written on a bit of paper in her wallet.

'That must have been from when she first came to visit me,' said Rachel. 'I know she'd been down about her daughter not wanting any contact, but I thought she had sort of accepted it, you know.' She hesitated, not sure she wanted to say the words out aloud.

'Was it accidental or...' her voice faded.

'We don't know yet,' the woman responded.

Later Rachel sat in Rima's flat, watching Amira playing, while Jamal slept in his mother's arms. Leah had loved Amira, she thought. She would get down on the floor with her and the two of them would play 'horsey' until Leah said horsey needed a nap. Rachel ate with Rima and Ali that night, the simple home-cooked meal with her friends providing some solace. Exhausted as she was, she didn't want to be alone.

Eventually, she went back to her flat. As she switched on the light, she glanced over at the area of the flat that had been Leah's. Just a corner really, a tiny portion of a small dark room in a little flat. Rachel sat on the mattress. Leah's few clothes were in a neat pile on one side of the bed, an old paperback book on the other side. She looked up, pulling something from the wall. It was a photo of the two of them that Lin had taken and given to them, Leah sticking it to the wall of her 'bedroom'. In the photo they were both laughing, arms around each other, Leah's spiky hair a brash purple that day.

As she stood up, she noticed an envelope peeking out from the mattress. She eased it out and looked inside — five one-hundred-dollar notes.

Rachel began to cry.

She would remember many things about her dear friend over the next few days: how she'd make Rachel a cup of tea in the morning, how she cared for her after hearing about Geoffrey, the games she made up to entertain Amira — but mostly she remembered the two of them learning to share a flat, the meals they shared, how they looked forward to seeing each other at the end of the day because it was so much better than coming home to an empty room.

Rachel clung to Rima and Lin at the funeral. She was touched to see Rosie had sent a garland of bright flowers; the colours of all the shades Leah's hair had been. There were few mourners. A couple of the cleaning staff Leah had worked with. Some faces Rachel recognised from the charities Leah had frequented like young Lucas.

There was no sign of Leah's children.

Afterwards, they went to the park with Amira in memory of the good times Leah had had there. The three of them watched Amira squealing with delight as she hurled herself down the slide, her little face lit up with pure joy.

'I wish we could stop time,' said Rachel, voicing what they were all thinking.

A week later, she ran into Robert.

'I heard about your friend Leah, I'm so sorry,' he said, looking at Rachel with such compassion she felt her eyes well up. 'It must have come as quite a shock.'

'It was. She'd become so important to me; we'd grown very close.' Rachel dabbed her eyes with her hanky. 'And I admired her, she was doing so well, it's such a waste. I feel so—' she said.

'Don't say you feel guilty,' said Robert looking at her with genuine concern.

Rachel looked up at him. 'How did you know I was going to say that?' she asked.

'It's a fairly typical reaction, especially given how close you were.'

'Her death was ruled an accidental overdose, but I'm not much of a friend, I didn't even know she was using again!' Rachel said starting to feel overwrought again.

'Rachel,' said Robert, putting a hand on her shoulder. 'You're such a good kind person, look at how you took her in? But sometimes, no matter how close you are to someone, they will only show you what they want you to see. We know there are always other emotions, other demons bubbling beneath the surface.'

'You sound so wise,' Rachel answered, smiling at him.

'No, not wise, just old,' said Robert ruefully.

They both laughed, their eyes meeting for the briefest of moments before she looked away.

She tried to explain her feelings to Rosie that night.

'It's weird, we've only had a handful of conversations, but he is so easy to talk to and...'

'What?'

'Well, I find myself thinking about him.'

Chapter Fourteen

Rachel looked at the clock. Three am. Great, she thought, the first day at a new job, and I can't sleep. Not that she'd been confident of getting any sleep when she went to bed. She was a ball of emotions — nerves, excitement, relief, and sheer terror. It felt like she'd been tossing and turning for hours. If Leah was here and awake, they'd share a cup of tea, Rachel thought sadly.

She had a job! And not just any job, a full-time job. It was the best thing that had happened to her in a very long time. Finally, she got a break.

The job was full-time administration assistant to the office manager at SalesPlus, a technology company in Parramatta.

When she thought back to the interview, she felt a strange mixture of shame and pride.

It had been a Thursday afternoon when she'd attended an interview with the human resources manager and the office manager.

The human resources manager was a young woman in her late twenties called Maddie Taylor. She radiated efficiency, working steadily through the list of questions she had in front of her. She had straight honey blond hair and large horn-rimmed glasses, the serious expression on her face never changing once during the interview. The office manager was more relaxed Rachel thought. She was an older woman, maybe mid-forties, Beverley Grayson (call me Bev, she'd said when they shook hands). She had curly brown hair and was wearing a black dress with a bright red skivvy and matching red lipstick.

Maddie had just asked her, 'What motivates you?'

Rachel had prepared for this question, but Maddie was looking at her with such a serious expression it seemed to put her off, and everything went out of her head. She felt herself start to mumble, Maddie staring at her expectantly behind her glasses.

Then, something snapped inside Rachel.

'I want this job. No, I need this job. I'm fifty-seven. I've applied for hundreds of jobs. Most of the time, I don't even get a response. When I am interviewed, they take one look at my grey hair and second-hand clothes and dismiss me. I've been told I'm too experienced, that I don't "fit in," when what they really mean is that I'm too old. I've been told I don't have enough experience, but how can I gain it? I can do this job; I know I can.'

I should stop, Rachel thought, this isn't going to get me the job, but it was as if something had been triggered inside her — the knockbacks, the rejections, the disappointments — and the words continued to tumble.

'Do you have any idea how many times I've been asked what motivates me? What I want to tell them is that being able to buy groceries motivates me, as does being able to pay my electricity bill and being able to afford things that everyone else seems to take for granted. That is the most motivating thing I can think of!'

Later, Rachel remembered that at this point Maddie looked slightly terrified, unsure of what to do in the face of such raw unbridled emotion.

Rachel's cheeks flushed as a single tear ran down her cheek. 'I'm sorry,' she said quietly as she stood up to leave.

Bev had been watching Rachel carefully. She already knew that Maddie had mentally rejected her for the job. She was a good HR practitioner when it came to things like policies and procedures, and talking about values and competencies, thought Bev wryly, but round holes, square pegs were not Maddie's forte.

But there was something special about this woman, Bev thought. For starters, she had been brutally honest. Bev had done a lot of interviews in her time, and it was refreshing not to hear the same old rehearsed pat answers to questions.

'Wait, you don't have to leave,' Bev said.

Rachel paused, glancing at Maddie, who remained speechless.

Bev pushed the papers in front of her and Maddie aside, as if removing a barrier.

'Now, why don't you tell us about yourself, Rachel?'

'We're not a charity,' said Maddie later, in what Bev privately referred to as her school prefect voice, when Bev said she wanted to give Rachel a go.

'Thanks, Maddie, I am aware SalesPlus is not a charity,' said Bev in her usual no-nonsense manner. 'But I think Rachel would be a hard worker and that's what I need.'

'Her computer skills are—'

'Lacking, beyond par, inadequate? I agree, but the basics are there, and we can train her,' said Bev. 'She has the right motivation and attitude, and haven't you always said that's the most important value SalesPlus wants in its employees? And we need to look beyond her age.' Bev knew she shouldn't be accusing her colleague of discrimination, but she had a feeling the young HR manager was struggling because Rachel didn't *look* like any of the other SalesPlus staff.

'I want to hire her. Can you please do the references and make the offer?' Bev said in a voice that meant the matter was now closed.

Later when Rachel got to know Bev better, she got up the nerve to ask about the interview and her outburst.

'To be honest, it was refreshing,' Bev told her. 'Sometimes interviews can be very formal, too formal, and I've often thought it's hard to see the real person through all those prescriptive questions and answers. What I saw was a real person who badly wanted this job, and who I reckoned could do the job. That was good enough for me.'

She smiled at Rachel, 'although I did have to convince Human Resources,' with a wink that told Rachel it was not the first time they'd batted heads.

She'd danced around the flat after receiving the phone call informing her she had been successful. She'd cried with joy, yelled, laughed.

A weight had been lifted from her shoulders: the feelings of low self-esteem, loss of confidence; of being separated from society. It had been part of her makeup for so long.

Maybe I won't feel those things anymore, maybe this is the turning point.

Her friends had been equally ecstatic. Rosie had yelled into the phone so loud she had to turn the phone away from her ear. Rima hugged her saying she was going to put on a special celebration for her. Amira had taken out her crayons, drawing a picture (smeared with butter) of a bright, yellow-coloured Rachel with a banana as a head entering a big purple building called Job. Lin had presented her with a gift voucher so she could buy herself something new!

Despite her sleepless night, she was pleased with her appearance when she gave herself a final check before heading to the station. She'd purchased new black shoes with Lin's voucher and was dressed in the golden silk shirt Lin had given her. Even with her worn black trousers, she looked very professional. She'd finally parted ways with her old brown bag and (on Rosie's advice) bought a new black one from the op shop.

Taking her seat on the train, she smiled as she looked around at her fellow commuters. Despite the butterflies in her stomach, she hadn't felt this good in a long time.

I belong, I'm one of you!

'I'll take you through our Corporate Induction and Onboarding,' said Maddie, the serious human resources manager she'd met at the interview.

Rachel looked at her blankly. She remembered the term 'induction' but what on earth was 'onboarding'?

'Onboarding is the SalesPlus process of introducing our newly hired employees to the expectations, behaviours and culture of SalesPlus,' explained Maddie.

Rachel thought this probably wouldn't be the last time Maddie would have to explain something to her. She seemed to be speaking a different language!

'So first I'm going to show you how to log in to our employee portal called PeoplePlus and take you through what you need to do. Along with the forms you need to complete, it will cover workplace health and safety, fire and emergency management, equity and diversity, and compliance-related topics.'

Without waiting for Rachel to respond, Maddie turned her laptop towards Rachel so she could see, her fingers moving quickly across the keyboard, telling Rachel to write down her allocated username and password.

For a moment Rachel froze, the familiar feelings of self-doubt starting to overwhelm her. She thought back to other jobs she started when a so-called 'induction' had been a hello from the manager and a vague sweep of the hand to indicate where the toilets were.

Reason kicked in — after being out of the workforce for so long, she was bound to feel a bit daunted she thought, as she wrote everything down carefully, knowing when she got back to her desk she could work through it all at her own pace.

Next was a tour of the office. It was the most modern office she'd ever worked in. Clean, fresh-looking, sparkling white surfaces. Lots of light.

The office kitchen was almost the size of her entire flat. It had a big table in the centre, where employees sat having a coffee or lunch, scrolling through their phones, or looking at their iPads. The coffee machine was a stainless-steel behemoth that seemed to dominate the area. It looked like a fat Buddha holding court and indeed was treated with almost the same religious reverence. 'Just like having our own barista,' said one of her new colleagues.

The first time Rachel felt confident enough to get up from her desk and go to the kitchen, she'd taken a deep breath and tried to walk with an air of purpose. She'd stood in front of the machine dumbfounded. Espresso, froth, cappuccino, lattes. A multitude of sparkling silver buttons stared back at her. Panicking, she quickly grabbed a glass of water, hoping anyone watching her would think that was what she'd been wanting all along. She made a mental note to ask Bev to show her how the contraption worked. Perhaps I'll just bring a small jar of Nescafe in the meantime, thought Rachel.

Her new colleagues fascinated her. As part of her 'onboarding', she learnt the other people who worked at SalesPlus were a mixture of software developers, salespeople, marketing, IT, and finance people. The developers all sat together. They seemed a quiet bunch, staring at their keyboards most of them wearing headphones. The salespeople were louder and formed a noisy hub in the office.

The CEO didn't seem old enough to run a company. He was in his early forties and from what Bev said he was hard but fair.

'He gets results and that's what it's all about, isn't it?' said Bev. 'But he cares about the employees, he's very fair to people, and he's very approachable.'

Rachel didn't know about that; she was too intimidated to do anything other than reply to him when he passed her desk and greeted her. But as she got to know other staff, they all seemed to like him.

The SalesPlus dress code was different to what she was used to. For some reason, she'd expected everyone to be wearing corporate-like suits but instead, everyone's attire was very casual albeit (to her untrained eye) mostly designer casual! The salespeople were more dressed up she thought, but not in suits, instead wearing chinos with shirts and smart shoes. The developers always looked very comfy in their jeans and slogan t-shirts.

To her, most of the girls in the office looked like models. A lot of them trooped off to the gym during their lunch break, arriving back in full make-up, not a sweat bead among them. Everything they wore seemed to be the latest in fashion, and if the number of parcels that arrived at the office were any indication, they spent a good proportion of their salary shopping online.

Chapter Fifteen

'**D**o you know you're the oldest employee we have?'

Katie was the HR officer who reported to the serious Maddie. Always smiling, her dark hair swept casually into a messy bun, she was a noticeable presence in the office; every time Rachel saw her, she was sitting on someone's desk or in the kitchen talking to someone. She was also exceedingly helpful, as Rachel gratefully discovered on many an occasion.

'Um, really?' said Rachel unsure of what response was required.

'I think it's great. Well done you,' Katie high fived her, a big grin on her freckled face. 'Got to go, bye!'

Rachel nodded her head while smiling bemusedly, unsure why she was being congratulated.

That was the first of many conversations she had where she realised the extent of the generation gap between her and most of her colleagues.

She hadn't known whether to laugh or cry when she asked someone if there was a fax machine, and the person replied, 'What's a fax machine?'

In return, her colleagues took great delight in showing her what TikTok was (she never let on that she thought it was a watch brand).

Lunch was a challenge. On her first day she visited the food hall on the ground floor of the Westfield shopping centre and headed straight for a sandwich place.

'Could I have a ham, cheese and tomato sandwich please?'

As she waited, she was amazed to see people having large burgers for lunch, or plates piled high with noodles or curries.

Opening her wallet, she asked 'How much is that?'

Handing over her money, the man looked at it and said in a bored voice, 'It's $9.90.'

Flustered, she scrambled to find two two-dollar coins, 'Sorry' she muttered, 'I thought you said $5.90.'

She was shocked. Five of those a week would break her carefully managed budget! From that day she decided to bring her lunch from home, either a sandwich or a cup-a-soup and crackers.

In her first month, she attended a session on values and culture. She'd never participated in anything like it before. They all broke into groups and talked about things like diversity, equity, inclusion, cohesiveness, resiliency. Rachel hardly said a word.

Maddie discussed SalesPlus behaviours and competencies. When she talked about how employees should behave at work, she looked and sounded a bit like a headmistress, thought Rachel, what with her stern look, peering over her glasses.

The first couple of months passed in a blur. As the days went on, she became more confident and was pleased to find she was enjoying the role. There was no receptionist at SalesPlus but the way the office was configured, with her desk and that of Bev's in a little alcove near the glass doors emblazoned with their logo, part of her job was welcoming any visitors and dealing with couriers. She made sure the hand sanitiser was always full and visitors signed in and out. Once Bev had shown her how to use the coffee machine, she became adept at producing whatever coffee any of their visitors wanted. One of the sales team had even passed on to her that his prospective client said the cappuccino she'd made was the best he'd ever had! She also got to know many of the couriers and looked forward to their friendly banter.

Her job was varied. She looked after the four meeting rooms — amusingly named Star Wars, Harry Potter, Game of Thrones, Marvel — which were frequently occupied especially by the sales team. She hadn't known what a 'quiet room' was until she joined SalesPlus. But a lot of people seemed to use the two the office had, going in there for respite from the busy, often very loud, open plan office. Her job was also to make sure these rooms were kept clean and tidy. These rooms were designed for comfort, and she often saw staff members in there, headphones on, gazing at their laptops while lolling on the lurid orange beanbags.

She helped organise meetings, did the stationery orders, looked after office supplies and a load of other tasks Bev needed help with. If any of the different teams needed an extra pair of hands, she was summoned to help. She liked that she got to know the marketing team when they were launching a new campaign, and the finance team when they needed extra photocopying done.

Not only did she manage her own calendar online but that of all the meeting rooms. While other people may have scoffed at feeling a sense of achievement for something so menial, she was proud of the responsibility she had.

She made mistakes. 'I was sure I was going to be sacked!' she'd told Rosie one night after she'd forgotten to order catering for a meeting.

But she was willing to do any task asked of her, no matter how menial. She quickly made herself indispensable.

'You know, Rachel, I don't know how we managed before you came along,' Bev said to her one Friday afternoon after a particularly busy day.

Her weekends also improved. Before getting the job, Saturday and Sunday had been just another two days like any other, with hours to be filled. Now she enjoyed a lie-in on Saturday morning, knowing it was a true reward for a week of hard work. Sometimes she would walk to the shops, buy a newspaper, and have a coffee out. She'd been able to buy a small second-hand television and a bright coloured throw for the couch along with a couple of plump cushions. The flat was becoming more of a home. At night, when she relaxed on the couch watching the television, she'd think of Leah.

She saw plenty of Rima, Ali, and the children too. They'd go to the park together or share a meal. And she and Lin had got into the habit of going to the movies together. She was surprised to find Lin loved action movies, and she had dragged Rachel to see the latest Fast & Furious offerings. Rachel had never seen one before and was surprised that she quite enjoyed it. She wondered what people thought about her and Lin — they were the oldest in the cinema — cackling together while they shared a large popcorn.

One Sunday when she was leaving the supermarket, she ran into Robert. Her tummy did a funny little flip-flop when he greeted her warmly, 'Rachel, nice to see you.'

Rachel thought there were two types of people in the world. Some only said things like 'nice to see you' because it was a social convention and then there were others like Robert, with his crinkly eyes and friendly face, who looked like they genuinely meant it.

He was delighted when she told him about her new job, and she was about to ask him about his job when a car horn startled her. Robert turned around, 'Rachel, I'm sorry I have to go, that's my son.'

Wishing her a hasty goodbye, she watched him get into a car driven by a younger version of Robert, the two of them laughing together. She watched them wistfully as they drove off.

'It's the low hanging fruit,' said one of the sales team.

'Okay, we'll take that offline,' nodded the sales director.

As she spoke Rachel studied her. She was very polished, she thought, and obviously highly respected. Standing at the front of the room Rachel noticed how the black suit perfectly moulded her tall frame, her short hair framing her beautifully made-up face.

Rachel had been asked to attend the weekly sales meeting and was noting down any agreed actions or things that needed following up. Her pen poised, she realised with a start that no matter how much the sales director commanded attention, Rachel had no idea what they were talking about. Hoping her face hid her confusion, she decided she would write everything down word-for-word and check with Bev later as to what it all meant.

The sales director was talking again. 'We need to be careful here. While I like that you're thinking outside the box, we don't have the bandwidth to do everything. So, some of these ideas we have to circle back to.'

The meeting ended shortly after, leaving Rachel feeling again like everyone had been speaking a foreign language.

On the train home that night, thinking about the meeting, she wondered what her new colleagues thought of her.

Apart from being much older than them, there were other differences too. While she'd been able to add a couple of new items to her wardrobe, she knew she'd never be in the same league with some of her fashion-conscious workmates.

She was fascinated with how they spent their money. Some of them still lived at home so all their salary seemed to go on going out and buying clothes. Sometimes on a Monday morning, she'd be in the kitchen when the 'what did you do on the weekend?' conversations were going on — weekends away, restaurants, bars were always talked about.

And if they weren't going out, they seemed to have Uber Eats on speed dial. And streaming services! From what she gleaned from their conversations, a lot of them didn't own televisions, they just subscribed to a multitude of streaming services.

One of the Sales team was planning her wedding and Rachel was dizzy when she heard her say that they had a budget of $40,000!

But many were realistic saying they would probably never be able to afford to buy a house in Sydney, so why shouldn't they spend their money rather than saving for something that may never happen?

She shivered when she heard these conversations, reminding her how close she came to being homeless.

She was woefully behind when it came to social media too. She had a Facebook account but never posted on it (she'd only signed up after months of nagging from Rosie!). Some of the team seemed to spend a lot of their time scrolling Instagram and on Twitter.

They were much more outspoken than she was at their age. She admired their confidence; their ability to speak up, to grasp at opportunities rather than shy away from them. Though, as Bev once said to her, the downside of all that confidence, is that they wanted everything *now* — she'd confided in her that a couple of the salespeople were looking for other jobs because they believed they deserved a promotion even when they'd only been in the company six months and were still learning the products and the market.

Despite these differences, most people were friendly (some completely ignored her, probably thinking that befriending the lowest ranking person at SalesPlus would be a waste of time).

One afternoon she stifled a yawn as she walked past the kitchen area and heard one of the guys from finance say, 'Hey

Rachel, you look like you could use a coffee?' She'd turned to see a group of them standing around the coffee machine.

'Get him to make you a latte, they're the best,' said a pretty fair-haired girl.

Without waiting for an answer, he proceeded to make one for her. She didn't want to say she'd never tasted one before, so she smiled at them, putting down her photocopying on the benchtop.

'So, what do you think?' he said smiling at her as she took a sip. 'Is it not the best?'

'It sure is,' said Rachel thanking him.

And at that moment, feeling accepted by her new colleagues in her new job, it truly was.

Sydney was suddenly plunged into another COVID-19 lockdown.

Rachel was at her desk when the NSW Government announced that the lockdown would take effect from midnight that night.

Rachel was terrified. I'm going to lose my job she thought. SalesPlus aren't going to need an office administration if there's no one in the office! She saw the CEO and all the managers, including Bev, assemble in the boardroom.

All around her, her colleagues were huddled in groups talking or collecting their things together. They'd been through this before; they knew the drill.

Rachel looked at the screen. She couldn't concentrate, the words in front of her swam. Her hands were sweating. She saw Bev coming towards her. This is it thought Rachel. I'm going to lose my job. Back to square one.

'Let's have a chat,' said Bev.

Chapter Sixteen

That night Rachel looked around the flat a wide smile on her face. Look at me, she thought. In front of her was her work computer. Thanks to the SalesPlus IT Department and their endless patience she was connected and was able to access her emails and documents. She had been embarrassed to admit that not only did she not have a laptop, but she also didn't have an internet connection. They had taken it in their stride, giving her a dongle to use and giving her step-by-step instructions.

She may only be an administration assistant but at that moment she felt very successful, quietly triumphant at how far she had come.

Rachel had almost burst into tears when Bev advised her that SalesPlus wanted to keep her on. She could hardly speak; such was the force of the relief she felt. Rachel would have to use some of her leave, but Bev told her there was enough work to justify keeping her on.

'Hopefully, the lockdown is only temporary,' she told Rachel. 'And let me add, everyone was very keen to see if we could keep you on,' she said with a smile.

That night she made sure she had access to the spreadsheets she had been asked to work on, ready for her to start working on in the morning. Then she popped next door to see how Rima and Ali were.

Rachel was standing at the doorway to Rima's flat trying to explain why she couldn't come in.

'The current rules are we're not supposed to visit people in their homes, so I really shouldn't come in.' Rachel had always been a stickler for following rules, a personality trait that made her the butt of many jokes from Rosie.

As in the previous lockdown, Rosie explained the rules to Rima. She also showed her where she could access information that had been translated into Arabic on the government website.

'And what about Ali, what about his job?' she asked Rima.

'He says it's okay for now, keeping him on, but fewer hours,' said Rima.

Once again, the two households would pool their food supplies and minimise their trips to the supermarket.

'Oh, hang on,' said Rachel, turning to go back into her unit.

She returned with a couple of apples. 'For Amira, for later.'

Wishing her friend goodnight with promises to see her tomorrow, Rachel looked at her phone. Rosie had sent her a lockdown meme along with an array of very Rosie-like emojis.

Early the next morning she and Rima donned their masks and hurried to the local supermarket for supplies. They were surprised to see several police patrolling the streets, some on horseback, the sound of a helicopter overhead. There was also a handful of Australian army personnel, brought in by the government to enforce the Covid safe rules in their community.

Beside her, she felt Rima shudder. She seemed to shrink.

'Are you okay Rima?' Rachel normally had to break into a jog to keep up with her, who walked as quickly as she talked. Now Rima was visibly pale and was eyeing the visitors nervously.

'Police and army on the streets in Aleppo meant trouble,' whispered Rima.

Rachel linked arms with her. 'It's different here, these people are trying to help, make sure people are using the QR codes and wearing masks. It's okay I promise,' she said soothingly although privately she too was amazed at the number of police and army personnel she could see.

When they got home, they realised why. Their suburban area had recorded the highest number of cases in Sydney. She, Rima, and Ali decided that they would take turns in going to the supermarket, and at the first sign of any symptoms, they would go and get tested. They'd already got their first vaccine.

As she got ready for bed that night after a productive day on her laptop, Rachel was once again struck by how much confidence she had gained in the last few months. She looked at her reflection in the mirror as she cleaned her teeth.

You've got this.

Her first meeting on Zoom had been another learning curve she managed to scale. She'd never heard of Zoom before SalesPlus but now here she was preparing for her first online meeting.

Bev came along first, waving to her from what looked like a sun-filled study, the wall behind her gleaming white with a small tidy bookshelf visible next to a sideboard adorned with neat piles of books, and a vase of fresh yellow flowers. Next came one of the sales team (Rachel was working on one of the sales worksheets), her face smiling as she showed Rachel and Bev the huge playroom she was conducting the meeting in; a long rustic looking table housing her laptop along with those of her two children who were doing their schooling online. Rachel saw glimpses of a swimming pool outside.

After the meeting, Rachel looked at the backdrop her colleagues would have seen – the dull brown wall, bits of peeling paint, unadorned with any pictures. She looked around wondering whether she could position herself somewhere else, but every wall was the same, and anyway she didn't have an extension cord. Perhaps if I could get a picture—stop, thought Rachel. You have a job. You're able to put food on the table. What does it matter what the walls look like?

But these things had a habit of niggling away at her, reminding her of the divide between her and others, sometimes hidden but sometimes in plain sight.

Like on a Zoom call.

Six months into the job, and no longer in lockdown, Rachel got a call from her mother's nursing home.

'She's deteriorating?' said Rachel quietly once the nurse had explained her mother's condition.

Rachel said she would come to Newcastle the next day and then went to look for Bev.

Bev was in her office peering at a spreadsheet on her computer.

'I don't understand how some people find it difficult to pass invoices to us on time,' she said gesturing to a pile of invoices in front of her.

She noticed Rachel's face. 'What's up? Are you okay?'

Rachel explained the situation.

'They think everything is starting to shut down,' said Rachel wiping a tear from her cheek.

'Do they...' Bev paused. 'Do they know how long?' she asked her eyes full of sympathy.

'No, I don't know. They weren't sure,' she said shaking her head. 'Sorry, I'm not making much sense.'

'That's okay,' said Bev patting her arm. She paused before she spoke again. 'When my mother died, it was one of the hardest things I've ever been through.'

And then she became business-like again. 'Now, what can we do to help you?'

As it was a Wednesday, it was agreed that Rachel would take the next two days off work as personal leave. Bev told her that she should keep her updated as to how her mother was.

She gave Rachel a cab charge to get home. 'No time to be waiting for Sydney trains when you're upset,' hugging Rachel. She also gave Rachel the details of the Employee Assistance Program should she need support. Rachel had no idea such a thing existed.

Over the next two days, her mother rallied, moving in and out of consciousness. Rachel hardly left her mother's room except to talk to Rosie.

As she sat holding her hand, her mind wandered. She wondered if her mother was thinking of her father. If she was, she hoped they were good thoughts, not sad or bitter ones.

She remembered how hard her mother had worked.

A birthday party popped into her mind. She must have been about eight. Her little school friends had loved the little party bags her mother had put together. Years later Rachel realised that her mother had had to work a lot of overtime to afford extras like those.

Her formal dress was lovingly made by her mother — Rosie had said it was better than any of the garish expensive taffeta numbers some of their snooty schoolmates wore.

Most of all, she was very glad her mum was spared knowing the truth about Geoffrey.

Rachel called Bev late on Friday afternoon, asking if she could have another personal leave day on Monday. Bev had brushed away the request, saying she should take whatever time she needed; she'd been more concerned with how Rachel was coping. When Rachel hung up she thought about how lucky she was to have landed the job. A couple of days away from it made her realise that she liked the job, the work, the people. She even missed her desk, the way she had organised it, made it her space, adding personal touches. Most of all, she was so happy she had someone like Bev as her manager. She knew from experience that it could have turned out much differently.

Her mother died three days later. Rachel had been with her, holding her hand, tears rolling down her face.

The following night, Rachel was heating some vegetable soup Rima had brought her for her dinner. Feeling drained, she paused to think about all the Sunday night meals she'd shared with her mum when she was growing up. Sunday nights 'we make do with whatever we have,' she'd say to Rachel smiling, which usually meant soup and toasted cheese sandwiches in front of the television. Rachel wiped a tear from her eyes. Her mum may not have been the woman she was before Rachel's dad had walked out on them, but she never stopped caring for her.

A knock on the door startled her out of her reverie. Puzzled, she dried her hands on a tea towel and opened the door.

'Surprise!'

Rosie.

'Rosie, oh my god, Rosie, what—'

'Are you going to let me in—'

They spoke at the same time, their words tumbling over each other.

It was a while before they were able to speak again; they hugged each other tightly, dancing around.

Finally, Rosie looked at Rachel. 'You didn't think I was going to let you cope with this on your own, did you?'

'Oh Rosie,' said Rachel and promptly burst into tears.

Chapter Seventeen

Later, as Rosie poured her a generous glass of wine from the bottle she had purchased (not long after she arrived, she ran out to the shops, saying dramatically, 'we need wine and chocolate'), Rachel studied her friend. The mop of hair escaping the bright bandana scarf. Her voluptuous curves in a tight yellow top underneath a black tunic she had paired with black leggings. Just looking at her boosted Rachel's spirits.

They stayed up until the early hours talking. Rosie was delighted her friend was doing so well in her job and was pleased she had lost the almost gaunt, haunted look she sometimes had.

Over the next couple of days Rosie was her rock; helping her to organise the funeral, and tackle the paperwork required. The funeral was small, just her and Rosie, Rima (Lin rang Rachel in tears saying she was sorry she couldn't be there to support her friend), and two staff members from the nursing home. As Rachel stared at her mother's coffin, she thought it wasn't much to show for a life. She instantly regretted the thought; her mother may have led a simple life in the eyes of many, but she had lived and worked as she wanted to, and the two of them had been a tight unit.

Afterwards, Rosie made sandwiches for them, while Rima cut pieces of cake she had made earlier. Rachel felt exhausted and worn out but her two friends wouldn't allow her to skip eating. She found it hard to chew but managed a sandwich and drank the soothing tea put in front of her. When Rima went home, she fell into bed.

The next day, Rosie and Rachel hugged each other tightly before Rosie went back to Melbourne. And Rachel went back to work thinking about something her mother used to say – 'nothing like hard work to keep the tears away.'

'Hey Rachel, everyone's going for drinks after work, do you want to join us?'

Katie, the ever-smiling bubbly HR officer was standing in front of her desk.

It was Friday afternoon, and all around her, the SalesPlus employees seemed to be winding down, a buzz around the office as weekend plans were discussed.

Rachel had been asked for drinks before but always made up an excuse. She liked her colleagues but to think she could go to a bar and make conversation with them was something way out of her comfort zone. But maybe...

Perhaps sensing Rachel's hesitancy, Bev chimed in. 'Sure, let's do it, what do you say, Rachel?'

'I'd love to,' she said, smiling. If Bev was going, she'd go too.

As Rachel tidied up her desk, she thought about how kind Bev was. When she returned to the office after her mother died, sitting on her desk was a beautiful, gift-wrapped basket. Bev had filled it with all sorts of things she knew she liked including peppermint tea, lavender hand cream, a scented candle, and Kit Kats. She was also touched that several people, including the CEO, had signed a card expressing their sympathy for her loss.

The bar was crowded when Bev and Rachel elbowed their way to their colleagues, spread out across a couple of tables near the back. The first thing Rachel noticed was how dark the bar seemed. The second thing was how noisy it was! She took in her surroundings — a cavernous space with industrial ceilings and mirrors on opposing walls, low hanging pendant lights and plush cream leather seating.

Next to her, Bev was scanning the menu. 'What would you like?' she asked, raising her voice over the din.

Rachel looked down at the menu. Thirteen dollars for a glass of Riesling! Rachel gulped.

'I think I'll only stay for one, so I'll get this one, you can buy me one another time,' Bev said.

Five minutes later, Rachel was sitting in one of the booths sipping her wine, which she had to admit was delicious.

She seemed to be the only one having wine. 'What's that you're having?' she pointed to the exotic looking drink Katie had in front of her.

'Espresso Martini,' said Katie. She pursed her lips in exaggerated appreciation. 'It's divine!'

For the next few minutes, Rachel struggled to hear Katie as she extolled the virtues of the bar they were in, how it was their regular and had been the source of many a hangover in the office.

As they were talking, Rachel noticed that Katie's phone beeped continuously.

'Someone's keen to get hold of you,' she said to the younger woman.

Katie looked at the latest message, a shadow crossing her face. She noticed Rachel watching her, and quickly rearranged her face into a smile.

'It's my boyfriend, he was just asking what time I'm leaving the pub, we're due to go out to dinner tonight,' she said.

'That sounds nice. Where are you going?'

Before Katie could answer, her phone rang. Glancing at it, Rachel saw the name Brandon flash up on the screen.

Katie pressed delete. 'I'm not going to be able to hear him in here,' she said, although Rachel noticed she again looked worried. The phone immediately rang again. And again. And again. And again. Katie, looking visibly paler, got up from the table and made her way out of the bar.

Rachel left shortly after, thanking Bev again for the drink and wishing her a good weekend. As she headed along the street, she noticed Katie leaning against a wall, her phone pressed to her ear. Even from a distance, she could see her face was streaked with tears, smudges of black mascara visible. As Rachel drew alongside her, Katie slightly turned her back to her but not before she heard her sobs. Rachel, uncertain as to whether she should wait until Katie finished the call to check she was okay, hovered. Just as she was deciding to wait, Katie turned on her heels and headed back to the pub. Rachel continued walking to the station but over the weekend whenever she thought of Katie there was a knot of anxiety in her stomach.

On Monday morning Rachel found herself scanning the open-plan office for any sign of Katie. By eleven am when her desk was still empty, she surmised that she wouldn't be in. Something was niggling at her; Katie could have a very reasonable excuse for not being at work, but the events of Friday night wouldn't leave her mind.

The next day Katie was back at her desk. It was a busy morning for Rachel. The CEO and the Sales Director were doing a major presentation in the boardroom, and she had been occupied making sure the room was perfect, the IT was all set up, and greeting the visitors. One of the visitors needed to make some urgent phone calls and needed a private space so she'd had to clear a quiet room. Then the weekly fruit basket for staff was delivered, and the vendor had raised a problem with her about an invoice. Finally, everyone was settled, and she had taken the coffee orders. She was busy at the coffee machine when Katie walked past her, water bottle in hand.

'Katie how are you feeling?' she asked. 'I looked for you yesterday.'

Katie kept her head down, filled her water bottle, and without stopping, muttered 'okay,' and went back to her desk.

Rachel was taken aback. Over the past few months, she and Katie had built up quite a rapport. They chatted most days. At first just about SalesPlus work, sometimes Rachel helped Katie with some administration if HR were particularly busy. But Katie's humour and sunny personality were infectious and most days they had a conversation or a laugh about something.

She wasn't hurt by the snub; she was more worried she had observed something on Friday Katie didn't want anyone to know about.

A few weeks later, Rachel was washing her hands in the bathroom when she heard what sounded like someone crying in one of the cubicles.

She immediately knew it was Katie.

Rachel hardly had any contact with her recently. Katie was going out of her way to ignore her. She never made eye contact if they passed each other in the corridor, and the days of Katie sitting on her desk having a chat were long gone.

Standing there listening to the girl's muffled cries, Rachel decided there and then to get to the bottom of what was going on.

Taking a deep breath, she said 'Katie, it's Rachel, I can hear you're upset—'

'Rachel, I'm fine. Please just leave me alone,' said Katie in a voice that sounded like she was anything but.

Rachel persisted, 'Is it your boyfriend? Is it Brandon?'

Since that Friday night and observing Katie in the office for weeks afterwards, if Rachel's instincts were right, something was not right in Katie's relationship with her boyfriend. And she was going to find out what it was.

Katie didn't answer. Rachel persisted. 'Katie, is it Brandon?'

After what seemed like an age, the cubicle door opened. Katie's pale face, puffy from crying, peered out. She gave a little nod.

Rachel held her breath. What she said next was important — if she was wrong, Katie would quite rightly be offended and angry that Rachel would even think such a thing. 'Does he hurt you?' she asked calmly.

So, I wasn't wrong, Rachel thought, but it gave her no satisfaction as Katie nodded and fell crying into Rachel's open arms.

Chapter Eighteen

Rachel took charge. She told Katie to quickly mop up her face and meet her in one of the meeting rooms that she knew was free. She let Bev know she was going to be away from her desk for an hour or so. Bev raised her eyebrows as she saw a tear-stained Katie hovering near the meeting room, mouthing, 'Is everything okay?'

Rachel quickly nodded and went to make two coffees — a black one for her and espresso for Katie ('can't live without them!' Katie had said to her on her first day).

Putting the coffees down on the table Rachel looked at Katie, who was biting her nails and fidgeting, before saying, 'I don't want to pry Katie, but I'm worried about you. I have been since that Friday.'

Katie said nothing, loosening her bun and then quickly twisting it back up again, tendrils of hair hanging over her red eyes.

'Why don't you sip your coffee?' said Rachel.

They sat in silence for a while. Rachel had no intention of telling Katie the whole story about Geoffrey. First, she didn't think she was capable enough and second, she didn't want to scare the poor girl. But Geoffrey had controlled her in the unhealthiest of ways and she wanted Katie to know that she wasn't alone.

'Katie, whatever is happening, it's not your fault you know,' she said slowly.

'He doesn't mean it,' said Katie.

Rachel waited, not saying anything in the hope that the silence would encourage Katie to speak further.

'He gets angry with me sometimes.'

'Why?'

'He doesn't like it when I go out,' responded Katie. 'Always wants to know where I am and when I'll be home.' She sighed and pushed a stray hair out of her eyes, suddenly looking much younger than twenty-six.

'Why doesn't he want you to go out?'

'I don't know. He gets jealous if I'm with my family or my girlfriends,' she said. 'Says he wants me all to himself. That's kind of romantic, isn't it?' she appealed to Rachel.

'No, Katie, that's not romantic, it's controlling,' Rachel said seriously. 'What do your friends and family think of him?'

'They like him I think,' she said. 'But they never see him when he's in one of his moods.'

As if speaking to herself she added defiantly, 'I'd never tell my mum and dad, they'd be so worried.'

'You said he sometimes hurt you?'

Rachel waited.

Katie nodded, and slowly slid up the sleeve of her long sleeve shirt revealing a bracelet of ugly bruises on her arm.

Rachel gasped, 'What happened?'

'I went to a Hen's Party on Saturday night. I got home about three am. I told him it was going to be a big night,' she paused before continuing, 'but he kept saying I was lying, that I wasn't with the girls but that I'd hooked up with someone!' She put her head in her hands. 'He grabbed my phone to look at my texts, and when I tried to get it back—'

'Yes?' prompted Rachel.

'He twisted my arm behind my back.' She started to sob.

'Oh Katie,' she moved to sit closer to her, putting an arm around her shoulder. Rachel took a deep breath. Not a natural sharer, it had taken her years to be able to talk about what she'd been through; and even now it was only Rosie, Rima and Lin who knew the whole story.

'I once had a relationship with someone who... liked to control me. There was a pattern: he didn't like me talking to my mother or my best friend, he'd get angry with me, then make me feel like it was all my fault, that he was only angry because of something I'd done,' said Rachel.

'Did you leave him?' asked Katie her eyes wide.

'Something like that. The point is Katie, it wasn't right, it wasn't healthy and it's not what a relationship should be—'

'He called me a slut the other day,' said Katie suddenly. 'Said my dress was too short, too low-cut,' she laughed but it was a hollow laugh. 'Me!' she said pointing to the plain black work trousers and shirt she was wearing. 'He's always making comments about what I'm wearing.'

Rachel sipped her coffee. 'One thing I learnt is, you can file it away and think it's a one-off, but it never is. Once it starts—'

Rachel looked at Katie directly. 'You deserve someone who treats you with love and respect, not someone who calls you a slut and gives you those bruises,' she said protectively. 'I can't tell you what to do,' continued Rachel, though I want to, she thought angrily. 'But I think you have to talk to someone, and you need to think seriously about whether this is the sort of relationship you want.'

They both had to get back to work, but not until Rachel had made Katie promise that she'd use the Employee Assistance Program and see a counsellor. As Rachel made to open the door, Katie grabbed her and gave her a quick hug. 'Thank you. I'm sorry I've been awful the last few weeks,' she said with tears in her eyes.

She hesitated before speaking again 'You would have been a great mum.'

Rachel was thriving.

Physically she had never felt better. She, Lin, and Rima had formed a little walking group. A few times a week early in the morning they would walk together, catching up and enjoying the quiet streets. If her knee played up, the other two accommodated her slower pace and the three of them would amble along together.

Sometimes on the weekend they would go farther afield. Once they had taken a train and a bus and walked the popular Bondi to Coogee coastal trail, the three of them in awe of the beaches. They had been like excited schoolgirls on the walk. Lin kept stopping to take selfies. Rima strode ahead, her shorter stature no match for her boundless energy, her hijab blowing in the wind behind her. Rima had, of course, bought a picnic for them, complete with a thermos of coffee, which they enjoyed sitting on a grassy bank looking out to the sea, surrounded by bikini-clad girls topping up their tan, small children and dogs scampering everywhere. The sea was the brightest of blue, the sun warm, the air carrying the voices of happy people enjoying the best Sydney had to offer. On the way home, they planned another day out to the Blue Mountains where they would tackle an easy bushwalk. Rima had already planned the food.

Rachel looked better too. When she looked in the mirror she didn't turn away in disgust. She didn't study herself in the mirror, finding fault with what she saw. She had been to a hairdresser and got her hair cut into a neat shoulder-length bob. She used a home dye to get rid of some of the grey hair. She'd started wearing a little foundation and had bought a soft rose-coloured lipstick.

Being able to afford to do a proper grocery shop meant she was eating better. She could eat vegetables and have a proper dinner every night. She'd pushed the packets of instant noodles she had stocked up on to the back of the cupboard. She felt it was tempting fate to have them visible.

The most significant change, however, was in herself. She had been lacking in self-esteem for such a long time. While she still went about her day feeling anxious, doubting and second-guessing herself, she also knew she was smiling more, starting each day with a purpose, and coming home at the end of the day knowing she'd worked hard and was good at her job. Seeing her bank account increase every fortnight when she was paid made her feel worthy again, like she was contributing to society.

Surely even her nemesis, the Federal Treasurer, would have been happy she was accumulating superannuation again.

Rachel's identity was now closely tied up with having a job; more than it had ever been in the past. SalesPlus had become like a family. She sometimes went for Friday drinks but more often she would have lunch with some of the finance team.

Amira had started kindergarten. Rachel accompanied Rima and the little girl when they went to buy the school uniform. Such excitement! Now her unit was filled with pictures she had drawn at school. Her favourite was the one of Rima, Rachel, and Lin out on a walk. The yellow ball of the sun was obscuring the green face of Lin, Rachel seemed to be a giant with huge orange clown feet, while Amira had depicted her mother as a tiny pink stick figure. Rachel loved it.

Rosie asked her tentatively one day whether, now that she was back on her feet, she had any thoughts about having a relationship.

Rachel had been surprised. 'Where on earth would I meet someone?' she laughed.

'Lots of ways—you could get a hobby, join a club, or even get on a dating app.'

'Rosie, I don't know—'

'I'm not nagging, you know I don't think you should jump on Tinder today,' she laughed. 'But after what you've been through... And what about Robert? You said you liked him.'

'Yeah, I know, and I do but, oh I don't know, I'm just enjoying what I have now, you know?' she said. 'I feel like I've come so far.'

'You sure have.'

When Rachel didn't say anything, she thought she'd lost her, that they'd been cut off.

'Are you still there Rachel?'

'I was just thinking. It's funny saying it out loud, but Rosie—'

'What?'

'I'm really happy.'

She made more improvements to the unit. A small dining table (adorned with a beautiful damask tablecloth Rima had made her), more cushions for the sofa, and a couple of decent pans.

Katie had given her a beautiful vase — a handmade coloured glass vase she said she had seen at a market and immediately thought of Rachel — which had pride and place on her dining table.

Katie.

Katie had finally left Brandon. It had taken her a couple of months for her to admit to herself that it was an unhealthy relationship. During that time Rachel had given Katie space. She didn't crowd her; she didn't keep asking Katie what was happening. She listened. She did however, keep encouraging Katie to speak to her parents.

It was a Monday morning when Katie appeared at her desk. Rachel looked up at her, once again startled by how thin she'd become, the toll of the last few months clear to see.

'You were right, Rachel, I spoke to Mum and Dad. I'm getting away from him,' she said quietly. 'They were so good, I thought they'd...you know...'

Rachel had grown very fond of Katie, and she was delighted to see the change in her. She was quite emotional when Katie gave her the vase. But she was completely taken aback when she received an email from Katie's mother, thanking her for the kindness and guidance she had shown her daughter.

Not long after, Katie left SalesPlus, deciding to move to Melbourne to make a new start.

Rachel even tried an Espresso Martini at her farewell!

Chapter Nineteen

While essentially her job was the same, she had been given different projects to work on and different company events to help organise. Bev tasked her with organising a Harmony Week event. Rachel learnt that Harmony Week celebrated Australia's cultural diversity, so she coordinated a big lunch where everyone bought in dishes representing their heritage — the kitchen had been bursting with everything from spicy curries and noodle dishes to homemade quiches, lamingtons and party pies. Rachel had come up with the idea of using music to celebrate different cultures. She'd corralled someone from the marketing team into helping her and the two of them created a fun playlist on Spotify; the SalesPlus office was alive to the sounds of samba, Bollywood, yodelling, indigenous music, African drumbeats, with a hint of Jimmy Barnes thrown in! The staff had loved it.

The CEO also wanted to start Tuesday breakfast meetings. So, every Tuesday she was charged with making sure there was a variety of healthy breakfasts options for all staff as the whole company got together for a weekly catch up. It meant for an early start, but she enjoyed doing it. It also enabled her to hear more about the business, most of which still bamboozled her, but she was interested to hear about the work everyone was doing.

When Bev mentioned they were organising a paper plane competition with Friday drinks she thought she'd misheard her manager.

'I thought so too,' said Bev laughing. 'But it's a young workforce here, most of the employees are aged between twenty-five and thirty-five,' she said. 'They want that social interaction.'

Rachel had been amazed to see the competitive spirit between them all; even the CEO could be seen carefully making his paper plane, debating its superiority with the developers who were too preoccupied with discussing the physics and projected gravity without actually getting round to making one.

SalesPlus had sent her on a couple of training courses, so her IT skills were the best they'd ever been. Bev even suggested to her that she might be interested in doing a TAFE Course. She had shown her a course — Certificate III in Business Administration — that she might like to do, and Rachel was giving it serious thought.

She couldn't believe how well everything was going.

What did John Lennon sing *'Life is what happens to you while you're busy making other plans?'*

AI Software was a large international sales software company, with offices in Australia, the United Kingdom, the United States and Singapore. They employed thousands of people and their slick advertising was everywhere. They were in another league to SalesPlus.

For weeks Rachel noticed there had been a lot of closed-door meetings at SalesPlus. This was quite a change as it was a very open plan set up, and a lot of meetings were held out in the open.

She hadn't given it too much thought until she started hearing rumours from some of her colleagues.

'If this happens, it will be good for us,' said one of the sales team, taking his energy drink out of the fridge.

Rachel was making herself a coffee and looked up.

'Why?' asked someone.

'These guys have got such a big share of the market, look at the resources they have.'

'Global company too,' said someone else. 'Imagine what that could mean for us!'

'Money's not an object for these guys,' a voice piped up. 'I've met a few of their guys at conferences, their bonus scheme is...' he whistled to make his point.

Rachel walked back to her desk, not sure what to think. When she broached the subject with Bev, she was equally in the dark.

Now, just a couple of months later, all SalesPlus employees were gathered waiting to be addressed by the CEO. The air was thick with expectation. Some people talking excitedly, others looking more pensive.

The first thing Rachel noticed was that the CEO looked uncharacteristically tense. She'd never seen him like this before. He always seemed so relaxed, so confident knowing he was admired and respected as owner and head of a flourishing business he had built from the ground up. Although he looked every inch the successful CEO in a crisp white shirt casually tucked into black designer jeans, today she could see patches of perspiration on his shirt as he scanned the room nervously, sometimes checking the large silver watch on his tanned arm.

Finally, he seemed ready to speak, and he had everyone's attention. He was flanked by the sales director; the finance manager, and Maddie, the HR manager who was looking (if it was possible) even more serious than usual.

'Over the past few months, I know there has been a lot of talk, some rumours about, and it's been no secret we've had a lot of meetings with AI Software. One thing we've always known is that the industry is small, and everyone knows everyone and, wow, haven't we learnt that all over again in the past few months?' he said and then waited until some of the noise had died down.

'So, I apologise if you've heard things second hand, but I wasn't in a position to speak to you until I had something definite to announce, and today I do,' he said.

He paused and seemed to gather himself before speaking again.

'I may get a little emotional.'

This seemed to make most of the SalesPlus staff sit up a little straighter and look intently at their boss.

'I think you all know how I feel about this company, and how I feel about all of you. Some of you have been with me since we started this wild ride, and some of you I've only got to know recently.'

Rachel started picking at her nails.

He looked up. 'As of this morning, SalesPlus has agreed to be acquired by AI Software.'

Someone started clapping; others started to ask each other questions; a few whistled; and some, like Rachel, were silent.

Maddie whispered something to Mark, and he nodded before turning to address the team again.

'I know you have lots of questions. And we're going to do our best to address them today. Before we do that, let me say this,' he paused. He had rehearsed this last night and again this morning, but it was so important he got it right.

'This wasn't an easy decision,' he began. 'When I started SalesPlus I had an idea, a vision. And a lot of youthful optimism,' he said smiling.

'I made mistakes, but I learned from them. In the early days, we grew too fast. We made some bad decisions, some bad hires. We scaled back, almost from scratch. I had some sleepless nights wondering how I was going to be able to pay people.

'What I am most proud of is this,' he stretched his arms out acknowledging everyone in front of him. 'We're here because of you — the best salespeople, the best developers, the best experts — finance, marketing, and the support staff who look after us.

'Being under the AI Software umbrella will bring its challenges there's no doubt about it. But it will bring rewards as well. We are now part of one of the most successful software companies in the world.'

With that everyone started clapping, even Rachel, although she was still confused as to what it all meant.

Maddie was now speaking.

'We're going to break up into teams now, your managers are going to start talking to you about what the next few months will look like — we have a roadmap that sets out a forward path for the transition.'

Rachel grimaced. Only Maddie could dampen what excitement there was with her gobbledygook.

Chapter Twenty

Bev and Rachel joined the finance team and listened to the finance manager, briefing his group.

'Are we going to lose our jobs?' asked Winnie from accounts payable as soon as everyone was seated.

Winnie was known for speaking her mind, and it was a good question thought Rachel. Even she noticed that while most of the SalesPlus team had greeted the announcement with excitement and enthusiasm, a lot of people hadn't, including the finance team. Perhaps, thought Rachel, it was because they were a different breed altogether to the confident brash sales team or the highly skilled and valued developers.

'AI Software and SalesPlus are about to enter into what is called a Transition Phase.'

There was silence.

'The SWAT Team is being assembled—'

'Um, sorry to interrupt but what's a SWAT Team,' asked Bev knowing that everyone was thinking the same thing. 'I mean, we know what a SWAT Team is in Police shows but...'

'The SWAT Team will be made up of representatives from both companies, as well as from the external consultancy engaged to help manage this.'

More silence.

'The external consultancy will be conducting a skills audit, and an assessment of the current structure in AI Software. From there, decisions will be made about the new structure.'

'Are we going to lose our jobs?' repeated Winnie.

The finance manager sighed and took off his glasses. 'The intention is that no one loses their job.'

Bev and Rachel looked at each other, both clocking the use of the word 'intention'.

'So should we start looking?' asked someone.

'We better get all our entitlements paid out,' said Winnie angrily.

He held up his hands to get everyone's attention.

'Everyone, come on, we need to take this a step at a time, the announcement was made today. We have to let the SWAT Team undertake their work. This is a wonderful opportunity.'

The faces in front of him did not share his optimism. They had heard a lot about the 'goodwill' that existed: that the intention was everyone would have a job. That they would be kept informed every step of the way.

But everyone left the meeting with more questions and doubts than when they'd walked into the meeting room.

Bev and Rachel went out for a coffee later in the day.

'What do you think is going to happen?' Rachel asked her manager.

'I'll be honest Rachel, I don't know,' she said. 'I know as much as you do. But I do know that the CEO truly cares for his employees, so he will do everything he can for us.'

Rachel was despondent on the way home. She was trying not to focus on the negatives; trying not to think of the 'what ifs? but all she could think of was exactly that — what if she lost this job? Even as she was telling herself not to focus on the negatives, she was doing sums in her head and planning what she could cut back on. Just in case.

As the weeks passed by, she began to feel almost invisible. The sales team were full of talk about getting trained in new products and being a part of lucrative bonus schemes. The marketing team were excited about working for a company that had access to some of the top tier advertising agencies in the country.

She was an administrative employee. She was in no doubt about her skills; they weren't special, they weren't unique.

The SalesPlus bubble she had felt secure in was going to burst, she could feel it.

A couple of the finance team had already resigned. Not willing to wait around while their fate was being decided, they had secured other jobs. Their empty desks were a daily visible reminder to Rachel that her days may be numbered.

The finance manager had been right, thought Rachel. The SWAT Team were certainly communicating regularly but what they did communicate seemed to result in more and more questions and more and more confusion. Words and phrases like 'skills alignment', 'roadmaps', 'time horizons,' 'learnings', 'cascading down', 'transition fatigue' abounded. But in terms of a simple answer to the question 'will I have a job?' the silence was deafening.

It was incredibly unsettling.

Finally, after weeks of uncertainty, it was announced the job roles had all been finalised and everyone would have an individual meeting with an HR representative.

When Rachel came out of her meeting, the office was almost deserted. Most of the sales team had gone out for a long lunch together, perhaps to celebrate their good fortune. The CEO was already ensconced in the AI Software offices at Barangaroo. The finance manager was in a meeting room with the remaining members of his team, all of them studying their screens intently.

She idly noticed there were a lot of dirty cups and glasses she'd have to clean up later; before suddenly realising that it wasn't her job.

Not anymore.

Bev was waiting for her. 'I'm sorry, Rachel,' she said sounding remorseful. 'I wish the decision had been different.'

Maddie came and stood beside Rachel. 'Don't forget, please contact me if any of the information doesn't make sense.' Rachel was surprised when Maddie gave her a quick hug before walking away.

Rachel started packing up her things. Bev found her a plastic bag for her mug, a couple of magazines she had in her drawer. Some other bits and pieces.

'You must use the Outplacement Services,' urged Bev.

At the meeting with HR, once she had taken in that she didn't have a job anymore, she struggled to take in what had been said. She vaguely recalled Maddie saying something about Outplacement Services helping her to find another job.

'They will help you with your resume, help you with your interview skills, and support you in getting another job,' said Bev.

Bev didn't like the expression on Rachel's face. It was closed, blank, like she had switched off.

'You have to call them, Rachel, set up a meeting. Promise me you'll do that?' Bev urged.

Rachel nodded.

When she got home, she didn't go in and see Rima even though she knew her friend would be waiting to hear what happened at the meeting. She ignored all of Rosie's texts. Instead, she sat in the dark. Then went to bed.

She stayed in bed until midday reliving the events from the day before.

Maddie told her she could work out the week if she wanted but Rachel said no, that if this was the decision, she just wanted to leave. Bev told her they would have a proper farewell lunch, that she would contact her and set something up. The way Rachel was feeling, she didn't think she could be bothered but Bev had always been kind to her so she just smiled and said, 'Sure, that would be nice.'

Her phone rang. Rosie. She pressed delete. It immediately rang again. Sighing, Rachel answered.

'Are you okay?' asked Rosie immediately.

Rachel briefly filled her in on the events from yesterday. For once, she was in no mood to chat with her friend. Her voice felt thick, her throat constricted; she didn't have the energy to speak any more than she had to.

A couple of days later when Rosie rang, Rachel got angry when she had inquired again about how the Outplacement Services support was going. When she admitted she hadn't gotten around to contacting them Rosie was astounded.

'But why? I know it's hard but these people—,' said Rosie.

'I'm not going to be lucky enough to be interviewed by another Bev you know,' cried Rachel.

'What do you mean?'

'Bev took a chance on me. She knew I didn't have all the skills, but she took a chance,' said Rachel. 'I'm not going to get that sort of luck again!'

'Rachel, I know it's—' said Rosie.

'Sorry Rosie, I can't do this now.'

It was the first time she had ever hung up on her friend.

Chapter Twenty-one

That night as she desultorily flicked a sponge across the kitchen bench, she came across the plastic lunchbox she had bought after she had joined SalesPlus. She'd sometimes pack a sandwich and an apple and sit at the big table in the kitchen enjoying the banter of her colleagues.

Rachel slid to the floor, her head in her hands, feeling the loss of a routine, contact with people. It was like she was in mourning she thought.

I used to have a purpose.

Rima, getting no answer to her frequent door knocking attempts, had taken to sliding notes under Rachel's door. The next evening, having just roused herself from the sofa, her hair flattened on one side, wearing tracksuit pants and an old t-shirt that was well past its use-by date, she knocked on Rima's door knowing she could not hide forever.

Rima hid her surprise at her appearance and gave her what Rachel used to call a Rima-special — a huge comforting jasmine scented enveloping hug.

Rima made her tea. Ali was sleeping as he was doing the night shift in a couple of hours, and Jamal was nestled on the couch napping.

'I lost that job, Rima,' said Rachel. She explained, with as much energy as she could muster, what had happened.

'Those people, do they know what they are doing? You are good worker! You changed so much in the last few months, you...' Rima paused to find the right words in English. 'You blossomed,' she said.

When Rachel didn't respond Rima said, 'You will find another job, I know you!' She hugged her again.

Rima made her promise she would look after herself and join her the next day taking Amira to the park.

Letting herself into her flat, she thought at least everyone else had faith in her, even if she didn't.

With the same dread she might feel if she was making an appointment to see a dentist, Rachel contacted the Outplacement Services consultant she had been allocated to, Marilyn Horvat.

She had read the glossy brochure given to her. She knew they were supposed to help her, that this should be a positive experience. But it was like everything since she left SalesPlus — she struggled to summon any enthusiasm; everything seemed harder, pointless.

When she was at SalesPlus she had taken care with what she wore. Now she tiredly put on her trusty black trousers and a pale-yellow shirt that did nothing for her complexion. She caught a glimpse of herself in the train window. The disappointment of being made redundant combined with the lack of eating over the past few days was etched all over her face. She thought back to when she used to get the train every day — was it only a couple of weeks ago? — and she'd be looking forward to the day, dressed as professionally as any of her fellow commuters, happily reading something on her phone or flipping through a magazine.

Marilyn Horvat was in her mid-forties, smartly dressed, and had an air of authority about her. She showed Rachel into a small room, framed testimonials on the wall *I got my confidence back and secured my dream job!*, a box of tissues placed discreetly on a corner shelf, along with a calming aroma from a small candle.

'So, Rachel, how are you doing after leaving SalesPlus?' asked Marilyn.

'Tired,' replied Rachel curtly.

To Marilyn's credit, she didn't bite.

'That's understandable. You're not alone in this. People lose jobs all the time. You'll feel a myriad of emotions,' said Marilyn.

Rachel said nothing.

'At SalesPlus, you were the administration assistant to the office manager. They spoke very highly of you,' said Marilyn looking at her notes.

'Not that highly, given I was let go,' responded Rachel quickly.

Marilyn looked up.

'Sorry,' said Rachel.

'You have nothing to be sorry about, it's perfectly natural,' she said. 'Have you heard of the seven stages of grief?'

'Sort of,' Rachel nodded.

'Job loss, especially a job which had become a big part of your life, can be devastating,' said Marilyn.

Marilyn stood up, picked up a black texter pen and moved to a small whiteboard.

She wrote 'Shock' on the whiteboard and turned to Rachel.

'You were shocked when you found out you were being let go, weren't you?'

Rachel nodded.

'When the shock wears off, pain sets in. You've left behind your colleagues, familiar tasks. You may start to feel angry — angry at the situation in which you find yourself.'

She wrote 'You don't deserve this!' on the noticeboard.

Again, Rachel nodded, surprised at how much her emotions were following the exact same pattern on the whiteboard.

'From there, sadness may set in,' said Marilyn, looking directly at Rachel.

'But this will — and I emphasise will — be followed by better feelings and the beginning of a new reality. The last stage, regaining hope that you can move on and get another job, is your goal,' said Marilyn sitting down again.

Rachel said nothing for a while, and Marilyn seemed happy to let the silence continue.

'Would you like me to take you through how we can help you?' asked Marilyn.

'Yes please,' said Rachel so quietly she was surprised Marilyn had heard her.

Marilyn placed a piece of paper in front of her, pen in hand, to take Rachel through the information. 'SalesPlus have paid for a package that includes a career assessment and advice on employment options. We'll work with you to update and tailor your resume and develop an action plan to help you get another job. How does that sound to you?'

Rachel clenched both of her fists and stared downcast. She knew Marilyn was only trying to help her, and she was grateful to SalesPlus for paying for the service, but she couldn't seem to think clearly. She just felt an overwhelming sense of anger, tiredness and lethargy.

They ended the meeting by agreeing that Rachel would email her resume to Marilyn as soon as she could. As she walked out,

Marilyn watched her with a concerned look on her face. She was used to meeting with people who were downhearted after losing their jobs but the vacant look on Rachel's face worried her.

The nights were the worst. The darkest hour was around 3 am. She'd finally fall into a fitful sleep at about 11 pm, then be wide awake a few hours later. What if I don't get another job? How will I pay the rent, the bills? The self-critical voices, doubts and fears swirled in her head. The scariest part, thought Rachel, which she hardly dared speak out loud, was that part of her didn't care; that while she had always found looking for a job a demoralising experience, she kept at it, despite all the setbacks and rejections. That zeal had deserted her.

Her self-esteem and confidence were plummeting. Again. All she felt was dread. Dark, all-encompassing dread. Dread for the next day, the next month, the next year. No matter what I do, it won't ever be enough, thought Rachel. Once again that feeling of being separated from society was gripping her. She was just a statistic now, another face in the crowd, another person sliding into unemployment.

Visiting the library again for job-seeking purposes felt odd. Rachel had loved visiting the library when she'd been working. She'd take her time browsing the books and magazines, sometimes stopping on the way home to sit in the park and read, the sun warming her. Now, it was back to the computers. Ground-hog day.

Chapter Twenty-two

Rachel had never been a big drinker. She always enjoyed the occasional glass of wine, but apart from one or two occasions when she and Rosie were younger and they drank too much cheap wine or Bacardi and cokes, she'd always kept herself in check. Not feeling in control was an anathema to Rachel's usual cautious, risk-averse approach to life. She'd also seen what drinking had done to Geoffrey's mood.

Today she felt different. From the moment she woke up, everything had been against her. She had run out of milk for her tea. There was no cereal anyway, so she had a dry cracker with black tea for her breakfast. She hadn't done the washing up for a few days, so every mug was coated with a slick of grime. The shoes she reached for to put on (a scuffed pair of black court shoes) had a loose heel. To walk in them would have been a recipe for disaster, so she put on her old trainers. When she got to the library there were no computers available, she would have to wait a couple of hours. On the way home (after deciding not to wait around) the rain pelted down. Her umbrella at home, she decided to make a run for it. Slipping on the wet pavement, she landed on her backside and if it wasn't for the people hurrying around her (no one stopped to help her) she would have just burst into tears there and then. Instead, she hobbled down the street, and it was only when she saw the lit sign of the bottle shop did she think — why bloody not?

Half an hour later, Rachel was dry, dressed in her oldest pyjamas, a bottle of cheap red wine in front of her. There was nothing for dinner, so she nibbled on a couple of dry crackers. She knew she would feel the effects the next day but at that moment she didn't care. Not about resumes, interviews, appointments. And at that moment, not even her friends. She wiped a tear from her cheek. She just wanted to be left alone. After a while, she turned off the lights and sat in the dark.

A few days later she awoke to the persistent ringing of her phone. Groaning she turned over, burying herself under the bed covers. The ringing started again, then abruptly stopped. A beep indicated she had a message. Rachel lifted her head wincing against the sun shining brightly into her room. With a sigh, she gingerly stretched one arm out to look at her phone, ignoring her throbbing head. It was 10.15 am. Rachel lifted herself to a sitting position, her mouth dry, a wave of nausea engulfing her, and listened to the message. *Hi Rachel, this is Marilyn Horvat, just checking everything is okay. We had a 9.30 am appointment so give me a call when you get this.*

A few months ago, Rachel would have been horrified and appalled at herself for missing an appointment. She tapped out a text message apologising, saying she had an upset stomach, then collapsed back onto the bed not giving the appointment another thought.

'How is the Outplacement going?'

A week after she missed her appointment, Rachel received a call from Bev.

'It's okay.'

'Marilyn said you'd missed an appointment,' said Bev.

Rachel was silent for a moment, wishing Bev would mind her own business, but then as SalesPlus were paying for the service, she supposed she had every right to ask.

'I wasn't feeling well, but I'm due to meet her again in a few days,' said Rachel.

'I know it's hard Rachel but they are trying to help. I know something will turn up for you.'

The call ended shortly after. Bev had tried to arrange a lunch date with Rachel, but Rachel was non-committal.

Rachel slept in most days, stayed in her pyjamas all day, watching television, or dozing on the sofa. She drank wine every night and lived on tea and crackers. The flat was untidy, in need of a thorough clean. She didn't know whether the unpleasant odour was her or the flat.

For her last appointment with Marilyn, she dressed in the same black trousers. Combing through a pile of dirty clothes she found a shirt that would just pass as presentable. She ran a brush through her hair and set off for the train.

Meanwhile, Marilyn Horvat had been reviewing Rachel's file. As this was the last allocated session in the package SalesPlus had paid for, Marilyn was concerned about the lack of progress.

As a seasoned professional used to getting results, what worried her most about Rachel was that, apart from the position at SalesPlus, her employment history was sketchy. It may take her a while to get something but Rachel sadly showed little sign of appreciating the dire situation she could find herself in.

'Hi Rachel, come in,' Marilyn greeted her, taking in the old blouse and slumped shoulders.

Once they were settled, Marilyn got straight to the point.

'Rachel this is your last session with us, so there's a lot I'd like to cover with you. Okay?'

After Rachel nodded, Marilyn continued.

'So now that you have your new resume, have you applied for any positions?'

Marilyn and one of her colleagues had reframed Rachel's resume, showcasing her experience and highlighting her skills. Rachel had to admit it looked much better.

Marilyn was looking at her, eyebrows raised, waiting for an answer.

'Um, no, not since the four jobs you helped me with,' replied Rachel.

Marilyn had been referred four different administrative positions and she had helped Rachel with the cover letter and application. Unfortunately, Rachel hadn't been successful in gaining an interview for any of them.

'What have you been doing to look? Have you been going to the library to use the computers?'

'Yes, every day,' she lied.

Marilyn gave Rachel a piercing look (did she know I was lying?) and said, 'It's always good to have a routine, a schedule. Perhaps spend a couple of hours each morning doing job searches online, then work on your applications after that.'

Marilyn used the remaining time to coach Rachel on improving her interview skills.

At the end of the session, Marilyn handed Rachel a handbook. 'This has a selection of interview questions, a lot of which we covered today.' She showed Rachel a couple of pages.

'See, there are suggested responses here, and a space for where you can tailor your responses or write down things that you think are important to include in your responses.'

'Thanks,' said Rachel. If Marilyn was disappointed in the lack of interest shown by Rachel, she didn't show it.

'Good luck Rachel, I think if you keep persevering the right job will come along. Just keep putting in the work,' she said.

When Rachel had gone, Marilyn wondered if she was right. In the short time she had known her, Rachel seemed broken. She needed to display more interest and enthusiasm if she was to impress a prospective employer. She sighed. Then turned her attention to reading about her next client, a middle manager with a finance background, who had been made redundant after twelve years and was considering a career change. There was no time to give Rachel any more thought.

Rosie was on the phone. 'You haven't been returning my calls,' she said as soon as Rachel picked up.

It was 12.30 pm on a Wednesday, and Rachel was sitting on the sofa in her pyjamas watching an old episode of Dr Phil. A large woman with a strong Texan accent had lost her life savings on an online romance scam, and she was about to come face to face with the perpetrator.

'Sorry I've been busy,' she said, watching the woman's son berate her for losing his inheritance.

'How's the job hunting going?' asked Rosie.

Realising she was not going to get to see who the scammer was, she sighed and switched the TV off.

'It's going, but nothing yet,' she responded.

'What are some of the jobs you've applied for?'

'What is this, an inquisition?' snapped Rachel.

Rosie didn't say anything.

'Sorry,' said Rachel.

'It's okay, just, you know, I wanted to see how it's going.'

'Well, it's not getting any easier. Look I have to go, I'll speak to you later,' said Rachel ending the call.

Rachel didn't know what was happening to her. All the people she had previously relied on for friendship, comfort, laughs — now she went out of her way to not only avoid those same people but be rude to them as well. She knew she was lashing out at Rosie whenever she called. She made excuses not to go walking with Lin and Rima. She still saw Rima, Ali, and the kids but she rarely went next door of her own accord.

Seven dollars. Rachel looked at the ATM screen and stared listlessly at the number in front of her. Her job seeker money was due in two days but most of that would go on rent. She'd have to seek help from a charity for food.

'I refuse to stand by and let you do this to yourself,' said Rosie, her voice rising.

'What?' said Rachel knowing she was being difficult.

She had been hiding herself away even more, not responding to phone calls, neglecting to look for a job.

'Lin called me,' said Rosie.

That silenced her.

Chapter Twenty-three

Rachel hadn't been surprised when Lin turned up at the flat. She hadn't responded to Lin's texts or phone message when she called to see if she wanted to go to the movies, Lin's treat.

Rachel reluctantly invited her in. Lin asked how she was doing and when she shrugged, Lin had glanced at the dirty coffee cups, the clothes on the floor, the empty wine bottle, the musty smell and let Rachel have it in her most direct manner.

'I know it's tough but stop feeling sorry for yourself.'

'You don't know what you're talking about,' Rachel shot back.

'Don't I?' challenged Lin. 'This isn't a competition about who has it baddest.'

Somewhere in Rachel's mind, she recalled that when Lin got angry or excited her English sometimes faltered.

She tried to interrupt but Lin was gathering steam. 'You lost your job — it's bad, it's hard. You lost your friend. You had all sorts of trouble with that man long time ago. But look at me, look at Rima, look out there,' said Lin, pointing outside. 'No one has it easy all the time, why are you throwing it all away?'

The flat was silent apart from the hum of traffic outside.

'I want you to leave,' whispered Rachel.

Lin moved towards Rachel, reaching out as if to hug her. 'We're your friends Rachel, we just want to help. Stop shutting us out.'

Rachel stood stock still, arms folded, looking down at the floor until Lin had no choice but to leave.

'She had no right to speak to me like that,' said Rachel.

'Get over yourself, Rachel,' said Rosie angrily. 'She had every right. You ignore phone calls and messages. Of course she was going to be angry at you. She was worried! We all are.'

'I'm fine,' said Rachel stubbornly.

'You're not. You're not looking for a job. Lin said the flat was a pigsty and you didn't look much better,' said Rosie.

'Charming,' said Rachel.

'It's called tough love Rachel,' said Rosie. 'We're your friends, of course she was going to ring me.'

Rachel said nothing.

'Rachel,' said Rosie softening her voice. 'I hate to be blunt, but you don't have a choice. You can't go on like this.'

The electricity had been cut off. Rachel didn't care. She'd got used to sitting in the dark. It suited her mood. She lived on crackers and the occasional bag of chips.

Maybe I'm going mad.

Rachel cocked her head to one side looking quizzically at Rima.

'You remember, I have to take Jamal to the doctor, you said you'd take Amira to the park,' said Rima looking uncomfortable.

It was 4 pm. A knock on the door had roused her from the sofa where she had spent most of the day.

Rachel rubbed her gritty eyes, vaguely remembering the conversation she'd had with Rima last week.

'Sorry,' she mumbled. 'Just let me grab my wallet and keys.'

'Right, let's go,' she said plastering a smile on her face.

Rima looked at Rachel doubtfully taking in her friend's pallor and greasy hair, the stained grey tracksuit, the large hole in the faded black t-shirt.

'Are you sure?' she asked her.

But Amira was already grabbing Rachel's hand, pulling her, keen to be on their way.

Rima handed a five-dollar note over to Rachel. 'Can you buy her an ice cream as well please?'

Rachel nodded, ashamed that she couldn't afford to buy Amira one herself like she'd done so many times before.

Amira skipped along happily beside Rachel. The sun was bright, making Rachel realise how long it was since she had been outside. She felt the beginnings of a headache. Thankfully she didn't have to say much, with Amira chattering non-stop beside her.

As always, the park was crowded, a blaze of colour and noise. Rachel sat down on one of the benches, yawning widely, as Amira ran to the climbing frame and joined the fray. Rachel smiled, noticing how Amira was dwarfed in her school uniform, the hem already caked in dirt as she jumped down from the climbing frame, her dark eyes wide with excitement.

Rachel stretched her arms above her, yawning again, stretching and turning her neck left and right, rubbing the muscles stiff from lying on the couch. It was a large park area, split into different sections. She could hear the cyclists riding around the busy cycle path, a group of high school students playing soccer on the oval. She looked longingly at people lounging in the shade under a thicket of trees, take away coffees in their hands.

'Auntie Rachel, my shoes!' Amira ran up to her, with shoelaces flapping. She waited for them to tied, her hand resting on Rachel's shoulder, then with a quick hug ran off again.

Rachel realised she'd missed the little girl, the chatter, the hugs. She yawned again, rubbing her eyes. Amira had made a friend, a little girl with blonde pigtails. The two of them were playing in the sandpit, sand flying everywhere.

The sun beating down, Rachel felt herself getting more and more sleepy. Thirsty too. Her stomach rumbled. She thought of the five-dollar note in her pocket. It wouldn't buy much but she could buy a muffin or something. She could say she lost the money.

Could she steal from her friend?

She glanced again at Amira. A little boy had joined them, and the three were carefully using sand buckets to transfer sand from one area to another, then jumping on the new piles giggling as they did so. Rachel swatted a fly away, the hum of the children's voices hypnotic.

Her leg twitched; something was biting her. She twitched again, slapping her ankle where an ant bite was slowly forming. Rachel rubbed her eyes with her fists. Suddenly she sat up. The sandpit was empty.

She jumped up, looking around her in panic. Amira was nowhere to be seen. She ran around the climbing frame, tripping over a stray toy, but couldn't spot her. She stood for a moment, her heart pounding, then looked at her phone, staring in horror when she realised she had been asleep for about twenty minutes. The little blonde girl with pigtails, Rachel thought suddenly. Rachel scanned the park, running towards the slides and the swings, but there was no sign of either her or Amira.

Rachel's breath quickened, her pulse racing as she ran one way, then another, darting around groups of children and parents. With growing horror, she looked back at the road they had crossed only a short time ago but which now felt like hours. Such was her state, she expected to hear sirens, but the road was quiet.

She gasped for breath, holding her side. 'Amira,' she yelled.

'Amira!' This time it was a scream and caught the attention of a group of young mums near her.

'Are you okay?' one of the women asked her.

'Amira, I can't find—'

'What does she look like? How old is she?' the young woman asked quickly, motioning to her friends.

'She's five, dark hair,' said Rachel helplessly. 'She's in her school uniform, green checked.'

'I'm sure she's fine, kids run off all the time,' said the woman kindly trying to reassure her. A couple of her friends, one holding a crying toddler, set off in different directions. Rachel ran the other way, the sounds of the women yelling 'Amira' in her ears.

She didn't how much time had passed — it felt like hours — until one of the young women rushed up to her.

'We couldn't see her,' the woman touched Rachel's arm. 'Could someone have come to pick her up or something?'

Rachel hadn't thought of that. Perhaps Rima or Ali had come by, seen Amira. Perhaps they had texted her. She quickly checked her phone for messages. Nothing.

Rachel screamed, wringing her hands, 'Amira!'

'When was the last time you saw her?' inquired someone.

'The sandbox. I'd... I fell asleep,' Rachel felt like collapsing, the enormity of what she'd done hitting her.

She felt rather than saw the disapproving looks, the women registering her dirty tracksuit pants and t-shirt.

'Where could she be?' cried Rachel. 'We've looked everywhere!'

She told them about the little girl and boy Amira had been playing with. Everyone spread out again, although not before she heard someone say, 'I think we need to call the police.'

This can't be happening, thought Rachel.

Chapter Twenty-four

Rachel moved towards a section of the park that had a path leading up to the main road. By now her head was spinning. Twice she almost vomited. What if she's fallen and hit her head? What if someone has taken her?

She was confused as she looked at the different play areas and sitting areas. She must have covered the area twice already but she couldn't be sure. She felt she was going around in blind circles. The women helping her were now standing in a huddle, having searched the whole area. They were holding their babies tight, keeping their children close.

'Rhys, stay here, don't you dare run off,' she heard one of them say as if losing a child was contagious.

With trembling hands, Rachel pulled out her phone and dialled 000.

'Do you want Police, Fire or Ambulance?'

'Police, please hurry.'

In a voice that seemed to belong to someone else, she said quickly, 'I need to report a lost child. We're at a park—' the words tumbling out.

Suddenly, out of the corner of her eye, she saw the woman who had first spoken to her, yelling, and waving to her. She was... smiling! Rachel turned to where she was pointing. Amira!

'Sorry, it's okay, we found her,' said Rachel, hanging up.

'Amira, are you all right?' Rachel sunk to her knees hugging the little girl tightly. Rachel looked at her, stroking her hair, checking for signs of any hurt.

A voice said, 'She's fine, I found her at the corner of the park, chasing this one.' Rachel looked up to see a woman in her thirties, a black Labrador by her side.

She tried to stand up but her legs were like jelly. The other woman helped her up, looking at her with concern.

'Thank you for finding her,' Rachel said weakly.

Amira had run off chasing the dog around, ending up at the corner of the park where it intersected with the road.

'She didn't go on the road,' said the woman as if reading her mind.

Rachel hugged Amira tight. 'Oh Amira, what a fright you gave me, you know you're not supposed to run off, love,' she said.

'But Auntie Rachel, I came to tell you I was going to take the doggy for a walk, but you were asleep,' said Amira still cuddling the dog.

Rachel hung her head. In a small voice, she said, 'Let's go home now. Say goodbye to the nice lady and the dog.'

'Ellie,' said Amira, 'that's what she's called.'

The woman smiled at Rachel. 'Don't beat yourself up.' She gathered the dog lead and said goodbye, leaving Rachel and Amira together.

Rachel held Amira's hand tight as she looked around for the women who helped her look for Amira, but the park was emptying, and she couldn't see them. A part of her was relieved that she didn't have to face them again.

Rachel's legs were still shaky as they set off for the short walk home. She gripped Amira's hand as she chattered happily about

Ellie the dog. 'Do you think Mama and Papa will let me have a dog Auntie Rachel?' Amira demanded. Instead of answering, Rachel ruffled Amira's head with as much energy as she could muster.

'Hello Baba,' a smiling Rima said, opening the door, smothering her daughter in a big hug.

Amira rushed past her (no doubt looking for food; she told Rachel on the way home that she could eat a cake the size of a cow, cat, horse, and elephant!) yelling 'I patted a dog, Mama, called Ellie, she licked my hand!'

'Baba, wash your hands now, come on.' Rima clapped her hands, laughing while she shooed her eldest child to wash her hands.

'I need to talk to you Rima,' said Rachel quietly just as Amira shouted, 'Auntie Rachel fell asleep, she was snoring like Papa,' as she ran into the bathroom giggling.

Rima looked bemused. 'Asleep, what nonsense are you talking Baba?' but then she took in Rachel's serious tone, the look on her face, her folded goose-bumped arms as if she was protecting herself.

'What happened?' demanded Rima.

Rachel had never seen her friend like this. She'd seen her upset and angry before, but this was different. Now, her eyes were dark and accusing, her body fizzing with anger.

Rachel spoke haltingly, telling her what happened. Rima's face never left hers. Tears ran down Rachel's face, but she knew she would get no sympathy.

'Please say something, Rima,' she whispered. 'I'm so sorry, you don't know how sorry I am,' she said pleading with her friend.

'I not speak to you now,' said Rima closing the door.

Back in her flat, Rachel wished Rima had yelled at her, screamed — anything would have been better than the awful seething look of indignation.

The electricity was still cut off, so she washed her face with cold water even though her body cried out for a hot shower. She couldn't seem to get warm. She found a couple of stale biscuits and went to bed, quietly sobbing with relief that nothing had happened to Amira; and the shame of what she had become.

Rachel stared at the sliver of light peeking through the window, thinking about the day before. She felt queasy through lack of sleep, and she had a headache, but after pulling on an old jumper she got to work.

Finding a crumpled plastic bag, she collected all the debris strewn across the flat — empty biscuit packets, tissues, bits of paper, used tea bags. She gathered the empty wine bottles and put them by the door ready to put in the recycling bin. She paused when she shook Rima's tablecloth and saw the stains.

As she washed the cups, she thought about her mother and all the hardships she had faced. She could almost hear her mother's stern voice telling her to pull herself together.

The little kitchen bin was overflowing, a nest of cockroaches had taken up residence. She got down on her hands and knees scouring the floor. Her back ached, her knees hurt; she wanted to feel pain, she deserved it. Sitting back on her heels, she spied the notebook Marilyn from the Outplacement Services had given her. Retrieving it from under a dirty tea towel, Rachel grimaced at the wine stains on the cover.

Next, she braved a cold shower. She scrubbed her face, washed her hair. Looking down she saw how scrawny and gaunt she had become. Shivering, she dressed in the only clean clothes she could find — a pair of jeans and an old top. Her hair still wet she boldly tackled her fringe. She found her old lipstick, liberally coating her cracked dry lips. For courage, she told herself.

Having hand-washed what underwear and light clothing she could, the bathroom now looked like a laundry. She opened every window she could hoping the fresh air would help clear the stale odour.

Grabbing her handbag, she headed for the library. Rachel hesitated outside Rima's flat. She badly wanted to talk to her friend, but she sensed Rima was not ready to see her. Forgiveness was not going to come easy.

Helen greeted her with a smile even though it had been weeks since she had been to the library. Rachel returned a watery smile.

The first thing she did was email Marilyn:

Hi Marilyn,

I hope this email finds you well. I want to first apologise. Losing the SalesPlus job hit me harder than I expected. I appreciated your help but realise I probably didn't show it at the time. I have found the notebook you gave me. I'm afraid I haven't even opened it. Anyway, I just wanted to say thank you.

Yours,

Rachel Farrowsworth

She then emailed Bev:

> *Hi Bev,*
>
> *How are you going? I'm sorry I haven't responded to your calls and texts. Things got a bit on top of me, but I feel better now. I'd really like to catch up so if you'd like to let me know.*
>
> *Rachel*

While she was typing, she saw Marilyn had already replied.

> *Hi Rachel,*
>
> *Lovely to hear from you. It says a lot that you have recognised how you were feeling, so well done! One of the most important things you can do now is to get back into a routine. As you know, we used up your allocated sessions but please don't hesitate to contact me via email if you have any questions about anything, I'm happy to help. Good luck!*
>
> *Take care*
>
> *Marilyn*
>
> *P.S. You should find the notebook useful but email me if you need clarification on anything.*

Rachel sat back in her chair, her eyes welling up.

She busied herself with emailing the cleaning company she had previously worked for, seeing if there were any shifts available. She then spent a good hour looking at her resume, at the changes Marilyn had helped her with. Doing a job search, she found a few part-time administrative positions, and a few full-time positions that, while she didn't have all the skills required, she did have some. She carefully crafted cover letters and tailored her resume accordingly.

Next, she logged on to the Energy Australia website and navigated to their Hardship Policy page. She'd have to request an extension for the payment of the bill and then call them later to see what it was going to cost her to get it switched on again.

After she logged off, Rachel didn't even stop to sit in her sunny spot in the library as she once would have done. She didn't think she deserved it.

Again, she hesitated in front of Rima's door but didn't stop. In the unit, she was pleased that the odour had improved. She closed the windows and sat down to call Rosie.

Chapter Twenty-five

Rachel wasn't sure what sort of reception she'd get when she decided to call Rosie. She'd been ignoring her calls and messages, and when they did talk, they'd often end up arguing. The blame lay fairly and squarely with her, of that Rachel was sure.

An hour later Rachel was emotionally spent; the strength and joy of a close female bond when you need it most can do that.

'We're going to lend you the money for the electricity bill,' said Rosie.

'Rosie, no, that's not—'

Her protests were in vain.

'You have no electricity, you're relying on food charity, you're only just making your rent. You never accept help, and now you're going to have to,' she said angrily.

'Thank you,' said Rachel. 'But that's not why I rang you.'

'Do not apologise to me again. I don't want to hear it!'

Rachel almost smiled; there was something comforting about being on the receiving end of Rosie's fury again.

'You're getting your shit together, finally!' said Rosie. 'But don't shut me out again, you mean too much to me.'

Rachel slowly and tearfully told her what happened at the park. Rosie didn't hide her horror at what could have been but she knew it would take a while for Rachel to forgive herself.

'Do you think Rima will speak to me again?' whispered Rachel.

She hesitated before she answered her friend. 'You've helped each other through so much, and you have a close bond, and the kids adore you — but give her space.'

Lin was, as usual, more direct.

'You were a bitch,' she said when Rachel called her.

Rachel was about to respond when Lin laughed, 'but I get it, we're just glad you're okay now.'

Over the next several weeks Rachel applied for pretty much anything she could, only to never hear back, or to receive a response from SEEK saying she was one of 500 applicants. She applied for jobs stacking shelves at Coles, Woolworths, and Aldi only to be rejected by all three.

Every night she went to bed, she reminded herself that she had a roof over her head and food (of a sort) on the table. But the old anxieties and aching lump in her stomach returned.

I just need another break.

Dusk. An eerie silence had settled over the streets usually humming with traffic noise and sirens. The silence was unnerving.

This was the first night of Sydney going into another lockdown due to COVID-19. Again. Rachel gazed out of the window. A couple of Uber drivers on their bikes were delivering food to impatient residents.

Rachel sighed. She must have applied for more than 200 jobs over the last few weeks. And still nothing. She pulled a face as she slurped her cup of instant noodles.

Putting her cup down she thought about Rima. Since that day at the park, they had barely spoken. Living next door meant they couldn't avoid each other forever. They'd passed each other, been polite; and for the sake of appearances, she'd hug Amira, the high-pitched squeals of 'Auntie Rachel' following her down the corridor. She wondered how they were doing given the latest lockdown announcement.

A knock on the door interrupted her thoughts. Wiping her hands on her jeans she opened the door.

Rima.

Rima was wearing a pale pink blouse that matched her hijab. Rachel didn't know whether to laugh, cry, or throw her hands around her.

It was Rima who spoke first.

'We're not allowed to come into other people's homes remember,' she said.

Rachel had to smile that Rima was now well versed in the lockdown rules.

'You know how sorry—'

Rima put her hand up, 'Rachel, please I know.' Rima seemed to be trying to find the right words. 'I know how sorry you are. I... maybe I overreacted, I don't know...it's just that if anything had happened to Amira...' her voice trailed off.

'I know, I can't believe I...there are no excuses,' said Rachel. 'I hope one day you and Ali will forgive me.'

Rima looked at Rachel, tears in her eyes. 'Islam teaches us that everybody makes mistakes in life. Of course we forgive you,' she said. 'You're family, we've missed you.'

With that, the two friends embraced, lockdown rules forgotten.

Rachel saw an advertisement in the local paper, Better Care Aged Care nursing home was looking for someone to work on their reception from 10 am-2 pm each day.

It's not full-time work but it's something, she thought. And she'd save on travel, noting it was located only a few streets away.

Uh-oh, she thought, with lockdown the library was closed.

Rosie.

She rang Rosie, gave her the login details to her email and together they worded a cover letter. Luckily, she previously sent her a copy of her updated resume, so all she had to do was attach it to the email.

'Thanks Rosie.'

'Fingers crossed for this one!' she replied.

Lockdown ended a week later. Rachel spent it like many Sydneysiders – hunkered down in her flat. She went for the occasional walk or visit to the supermarket. She was lucky that she had only recently borrowed a few library books. Usually, books were a great escape, and she could spend hours reading. But the combination of another COVID lockdown and her precarious financial situation meant she found it difficult to settle for long periods. She was restless, fidgety. She would check in with Rosie every day and had spoken to Lin. Lin was working from home and in her unique direct way, would tell Rachel what she thought about some of her colleagues ('they're stupid').

Rima was a stickler for the rules (households weren't meant to mix during lockdown) so Amira and Jamal would stand at their entrance way and wave and call out to their Auntie Rachel. It was hard going for Rima and Ali to explain to them why they couldn't go to the park. They shared food and worries. Rachel shivered when she thought back to the time when Rima wasn't in her life.

Rima and Rachel had both knocked on Mr Quan's door to see if he needed anything. Rachel was worried about the old couple; she had read enough to know what would happen if the old couple got the virus. They both wore their masks and kept their distance. With them yelling from a distance and Mr Quan responding in his broken English, they figured out what he needed and delivered a package to his doorstep later in the day.

'Hello, is that Rachel Farrowsworth?'

It was the first morning after the lockdown ended and Rachel was about to set off for the library to use the computer when her phone rang.

'Yes, speaking.'

Arjun Singh, the general manager of Better Care Aged Care was ringing to arrange an interview with her.

'When can you come in for an interview?' he asked.

'Well, anytime,' she said. 'Anytime that suits you. I can even come in today.'

Arjun seemed impressed that she was keen, and they arranged an interview for 2 pm.

Rachel abandoned her plans to go to the library.

First, she made sure her black trousers were clean. She laid them out of the sofa to get rid of any creases. She found the high-neck cream blouse that she'd worn when she got the SalesPlus job. She was fastidious about keeping it clean, so it was good to go. Finally, she rubbed her black court shoes with an old rag until they looked as good as new.

Second, she sat on the sofa and looked again at the advertisement: *Receptionist/Administration Officer Mon – Fri 10 am – 2 pm*. She remembered Marilyn told her to pick out the key elements of the job and to write them on a piece of paper. She found the notebook Marilyn had given her and found where an example of this was covered.

Being the first point of contact for residents, families, staff, volunteers, and visitors.

Ensure the COVID-19 visitor sign-in process is adhered to.

Answer phone calls/redirect calls, pass on accurate messages as required.

Assisting with creating resident new admission documents.

General office administrative duties as required.

Marilyn then advised her to write under each of the elements her specific experience in each area. This she did carefully. She also remembered something else that Marilyn had told her — that just because she may not have a certain job title on her resume (in this case receptionist) if she had done all the aspects of the job, she should highlight them at the interview. When she finished, she sat back and read what she had written. She'd always been thorough about preparing for interviews, but she now saw the value in what Marilyn had recommended.

As she walked there, she texted Rosie to tell her she was on her way to the interview. When her phone beeped she looked at Rosie's response in surprise. She'd expected a thumbs up emoji or similar, but this was a long text. She read it with interest.

She was interviewed by Arjun Singh and a woman called Vanessa who was the full-time receptionist. Arjun Singh was all business, and passionately committed to the nursing home he ran and the residents he cared for. She liked Vanessa immediately; she reminded her of Bev.

'It's quite a busy reception area and we've realised that at lunchtime we need an extra pair of hands,' Arjun was saying.

Rachel nodded as he continued. 'Plus, if Vanessa gets called away to help with something, we need to make sure we have coverage.'

Rachel felt she answered all their questions well. She described how she looked after all the visitors at SalesPlus; she filled them in on the staff events she helped organise; how proficient she was with administrative tasks.

Arjun was looking at her resume, 'You haven't worked at a nursing home before, have you?' he said looking up at her.

Thank you, Rosie, she said in her head. Rachel proceeded to tell Arjun and Vanessa that she had looked after her mother for a year, coordinating the care she needed; that she spent a lot of time at her mother's nursing home. She also mentioned Rima and Ali, and Mr and Mrs Quan and described what she did to help them.

When she finished, she thought Arjun and Vanessa looked happy with her responses; that even though she hadn't worked in a nursing home, she thought she had demonstrated enough of her caring nature and community-mindedness.

'If you were successful, when could you start?' Vanessa was asking.

'Straight away,' said Rachel smiling, her fingers tightly crossed.

Chapter Twenty-six

Rachel rang Rosie on the way home.

'You're a genius,' she said when Rosie answered. 'I didn't even think of telling them about those things, until your text.'

'Stick with me Rachel, we'll go places together,' she faked a bad American accent.

Rachel laughed and rolled her eyes, telling her she'd contact her straight away if she heard anything.

She then sent Bev a quick text saying she had put her down as a reference. Bev immediately responded with a thumbs up and good luck.

Two days later she was offered the job. The hourly rate was lower than what she had been on at SalesPlus and the job was only twenty hours a week. She made herself a cup of tea and sat down to do her sums.

It was tight. The government payment would be understandably reduced. Paying the rent was the priority. Once she bought her meagre food provisions there would be little left over. Even with the saving on travel.

Rachel put down her pen and sat back. Since she'd left SalesPlus she must have applied for over 300 jobs. She hadn't even come close to getting a full-time job. She had no choice but to take part-time work. Her frugal existence would have to continue and potentially get even more frugal — if that was possible, she thought ruefully.

At the back of her mind, she was worried about her emotional and mental health. The period after leaving SalesPlus proved to her (as if she had needed reminding) what having paid work meant to her. Without it, she felt cast off. Alone and vulnerable.

I don't want to go through that again.

She used to listen to some of the SalesPlus employees complaining about having to budget or cut back on their expenses.

'No Uber Eats this week for me if I'm to make it till payday.'

'I CANNOT buy any new clothes this week. If you see me online stop me!'

'Mate, I'll have a few drinks at the pub, but I can't have a big one. Pay day's not till next week.'

'I was going to go away this weekend, up the coast, but I better not.'

For me, it means only eating four out of seven days.

She also liked the idea of working at the nursing home, playing a small part in helping to look after people who needed it. Arjun and Vanessa had seemed nice. She knew she could easily do the job. And she liked what she'd seen of the nursing home. The home looked clean and bright, flowers dotted around the place, staff bustling around looking after their charges.

She would take the job. She would also start looking for some cleaning work. That had come to her in the night. She'd previously done casual cleaning work, but her sights had been fully set on securing full-time work — but now she didn't have that luxury of choice. Perhaps she could figure out how to get some cleaning shifts that she could fit around the nursing home job?

That afternoon she popped into the nursing home to sign her employment paperwork.

'It will be great to have you start with us Rachel,' said Vanessa.

'Thanks, Vanessa, I'm looking forward to it,' said Rachel.

'Well hello Margery,' Vanessa turned her attention to a tiny woman who was wheeling her walker towards the reception. She had tufts of silver hair on her head, arms like twigs, but her green eyes were bright. 'This is Rachel, she's going to be joining us Monday, helping me out.'

Margery walked right up to Rachel. 'Well, that's nice, you look bonny,' she said in a broad Scottish accent.

Rachel smiled at the old lady, 'You look bonny yourself Margery. I can't wait to start on Monday, and get to know you.'

Vanessa looked on approvingly. As Margery made her way slowly along the corridor. 'That was nice. You'd be surprised, a lot of people don't know how to talk to the elderly.'

They chatted for a few more minutes until Vanessa had to answer the phone. Rachel waved goodbye and went on her way. Vanessa clearly knew everyone in the home, and Rachel liked her friendly no-nonsense manner. With her easy smile, she could see why she'd be popular with both staff and residents.

She rang Rosie to tell her the good news, then went to see Rima.

'Rachel, I'm so happy for you, come in, come in,' her friend said when she told her the news.

Amira and Jamal were both trying to jump onto Auntie Rachel's lap. She manoeuvred both jiggling them on one knee each until her left knee begged for mercy.

'What shall we do to celebrate?' asked Rima clapping her hands.

'Park, ice cream,' yelled Amira.

'Ice cream,' echoed Jamal.

Rachel glanced at Rima. Every time 'park' was mentioned, Rachel felt another wave of shame and embarrassment.

But Rima had put it behind her so soon the two of them were wrangling the children down the street towards the park and the promise of ice cream for all.

Later, she called Lin to tell her. 'We're going to the movies this weekend, my treat, we celebrate,' said Lin before complaining to her about the latest transgressions committed by her colleagues.

'Then you just hold it up like this,' said Rachel showing a couple how to use their mobile phone to check into the nursing home via the Government's check-in app.

Rachel had been in the job for a week and was loving it. She and Vanessa worked well together, and it hadn't taken long for Vanessa to show her the relevant procedures and paperwork for Rachel to get the hang of it and know what she had to do. With COVID-19 there were a lot of rules and procedures in place and Rachel was careful to follow every step.

The staff were friendly. Rushed off their feet but always smiling and friendly. Most of the nurses and personal care workers were migrants from South-East Asia. They had tough jobs, but they did everything with such care and good humour, Rachel quickly found herself in awe of them.

Margery was a regular visitor to the reception area. As was Bob, who seemed to spend most of his time grumbling but enjoyed sitting watching the comings and goings. Thalia and Gaia, two

Greek ladies who were always together, were the resident gossips and enjoyed annoying Bob with their chatter.

Sometimes Rachel had to drop something off on the other floors. A lot of residents would sit in the light-filled lounge areas, some asleep, some staring blankly at the television, some sadly not capable of doing anything.

'Beth, where are you going, pet?' said Rachel to a slight woman clutching her yellow cardigan around her and looking confused.

The woman peered at Rachel. 'Where's my room gone?' her voice rising in distress.

'This way, come, you're going the wrong way, pet.' Rachel put the papers she was carrying under one arm, and tucked Beth's hand in hers, talking to her quietly until the lady calmed down. Rachel settled her in her chair and promised to get a cup of tea for her.

'Thanks Rachel,' said Pari, one of the care workers as she hurried past Rachel, quickly putting on some gloves as she entered the room next to Beth's.

That afternoon as Rachel walked home, she thought about her mother. She thought her mother would be proud of her doing this job. The thought cheered her.

The next day after her shift finished, she went and met with the operations team lead at Blitz Cleaning, the company she had previously worked for. They were a large commercial cleaning company and serviced a lot of workplaces (of all sizes) in South West Sydney, and she'd been on their books doing the occasional shift.

Craig was the team leader, a solid man in his forties. Originally from Newcastle in England, he and his wife had moved to Australia fifteen years ago. He liked a beer and punt; Rachel knew this because he told everyone who cared to listen about his Saturdays which were spent in a pub betting. Craig did all the rostering, and he was a fair man.

'I was sorry to hear about your friend Leah,' he said.

'Yes,' said Rachel. She still found it hard to talk about and she couldn't afford to break down in tears when she needed work.

'So, you're after shifts?' said Craig.

Rachel explained that she had a part-time role, and she was looking for more casual cleaning work.

Craig had often had to review Rachel's work and knew she was a good cleaner. More importantly, he knew she was reliable. Not like some who didn't bother showing up.

Craig was looking at his computer, flicking through work rosters.

Rachel took a deep breath. 'How was the weekend? You still go to The Station for a bet?'

With that, Craig was off, telling her about the betting club at the pub, and the fishing day he was organising for his fellow drinkers.

'Well, you've always been one of the most reliable casual cleaners we've had so I can throw a few regular shifts your way. Now tell me the days and times you can do, and we can get the ball rolling,' said Craig.

Chapter Twenty-seven

'You flirt Rachel!' teased Rosie that night when she rang to tell her the news.

Rachel laughed. 'Ha ha. It was just a case of subtly reminding him what an asset I am,' she said in a mocking voice. 'In fact, there's more good news.'

When Rachel was leaving, Craig asked her whether she'd heard about the new online *Cleaning for Infection Control Course.* He'd explained it covers methods for cleaning to prevent the spread of infection.

'As you're casual you'll have to pay for it yourself but it's worth doing,' Craig told her. 'It only takes thirty minutes online and it's cheap, but if you want more regular work, you should do it.'

'Well, it sounds like it will be worth it,' Rosie commented to Rachel.

'Definitely. If I can get regular cleaning work as well as the Better Care Aged Care work, I can start to get back to normal a bit,' said Rachel feeling a burst of optimism she hadn't felt for a while.

The next morning, she was bought back to earth with a thud. When she had woken her knee had been throbbing. She'd hobbled to the kitchen to get her tea wincing in pain with every step.

At that moment, she heard a familiar voice on the radio — her old friend the Federal Treasurer was again telling Australians they may have to work longer. This time, instead of scowling and rolling her eyes, she stopped short, sitting down on the sofa heavily.

How on earth was she going to do regular cleaning work (which on occasion was more like a gym session) when she could hardly walk from the bedroom to the kitchen?

But what choice did she have? The nursing home job was working out fine and she hoped it would continue that way. She was banking on being able to pick up extra hours there once she had proved herself. She would continue to apply for administration jobs but deep down she knew that the chances of her getting another office job were slim. Cleaning was going to be tough physically, but she needed to do it to make ends meet.

When it came around to the time she had to leave to get to the nursing home, her knee was feeling better. Sore but better. Maybe she would just have to make sure she had plenty of rest between shifts.

'Rachel, I didn't expect to see you here!'

She was sitting at the reception desk concentrating on completing some new resident admission paperwork.

When she looked up, she was startled to see Robert standing in front of her.

'Robert, hi,' she said patting her hair into place as she stood up. 'Are you here to see someone?'

'I take it you work here now?'

They spoke at the same time and laughed.

'You first,' said Rachel.

'I'm here to see my aunt, Vivian Martin,' said Robert.

'Oh yes, Vivian. I've met her, she's lovely,' said Rachel thinking of the spritely lady on Level Two who loved joining in the bingo. 'And yes, I work here now. Part-time, I've been here for a couple of months.'

As Robert signed in, Rachel checked the daily calendar of activities for the residents.

'Actually Robert, the bingo has just started in the lounge, I think that's where you'll find Vivian. And morning tea has just started — good timing!'

'Well, I hope it's the scones today,' said Robert lingering a while longer at the reception area.

'Friend of yours?' asked Vanessa when Robert walked away.

'Oh, not really, I just bump into him occasionally,' said Rachel.

'Then why are you blushing? Or hadn't you noticed how handsome he is,' teased Vanessa giggling.

Rachel knew her face was red. And yes, she had noticed. He looked even better today, sporting a slight tan, highlighted even more by the white linen shirt he was wearing.

When Robert finished his visit and was signing out, she asked how his aunt was.

'Well, I didn't get much of a look in, she told me in no uncertain terms I shouldn't visit when the bingo was on!' laughed Robert.

Vanessa and Rachel both laughed.

Robert seemed to hesitate before he spoke again.

'Actually Rachel, it would be nice to catch up properly over a coffee,' he said. 'I mean if you'd like to...'

'That sounds good,' she replied, also hesitating slightly.

Vanessa, listening in, decided she needed to move things along. They obviously liked each other, she thought, but at this rate they'd be having their first coffee date when they were both living in the nursing home.

'Rachel, why don't you finish early. It's quiet now and you did come in early today,' said Vanessa.

Rachel looked at her watch — 1.30 pm. And she had come in a bit early today to help set up the dining room as they were short-staffed. She looked at Robert. 'Well, if you're free...'

'Perfect timing,' said Robert.

'Thanks Vanessa, I appreciate it,' she said, picking up her bag.

'You enjoy yourself, love,' responded Vanessa, squeezing her arm.

Half an hour later Rachel and Robert were sitting at an outdoor table of a local café. The sun was shining, the streets bustling with people.

'How is it going? Do you like it?' asked Rachel after Robert told her that he got the job he had interviewed for months ago, writing sales tender documents for a technology company.

He thought before answering.

'Most days I do. But it's very different to the job in the public service I was doing before. I won't bore you with the details. The main thing is I have a job.' He shivered. 'I never want to go back to those days of being unemployed and getting rejected.'

Rachel nodded in agreement. In turn, she told him about SalesPlus.

'I was like a different person at that job,' she said. 'And when it was gone, well let's just say I didn't handle it very well.'

Robert looked concerned. 'What happened?' Then he quickly added, 'Actually, no don't tell me if you don't want to.'

'No, it's okay. Before SalesPlus, as hard as it was, I was very motivated about getting a job. I kept going, even after rejection after rejection I kept going. After SalesPlus, let's just say I found it a lot harder,' she said.

She didn't tell him about her drinking, how she rarely got out of bed, how badly she had treated her friends or about what happened at the park.

She didn't want to tell him just how far she had sunk.

'I didn't even take much notice of the Outplacement Services,' she said shaking her head as she remembered how stupid she was.

'Well, I don't think you're the first person to do that,' said Robert.

They sat in companionable silence enjoying the sun on their faces.

'Perhaps it's made you realise how important working is to you; not just to pay bills? I mean I can tell how much you like the job at the nursing home,' suggested Robert.

Rachel was not surprised by Robert's perceptiveness, but it gave her a pleasant jolt that he had articulated precisely how she was feeling.

'Yes, that's exactly it,' said Rachel. 'And I hadn't realised that before. A job has always been just a job. SalesPlus was different,' she took a sip of her coffee. 'I felt different. I need to work. I can't afford not to. If I don't work, I don't eat,' Rachel continued, deciding she was going to be truthful about her situation; she wasn't going to sugar coat it.

Robert was looking at her with something she hadn't seen from a man in a while. Perhaps never.

Admiration.

'We do what we have to do, I certainly didn't think I'd end up doing what I do now.'

'What did you want to do when you were growing up?' asked Rachel.

'Promise you won't laugh?' asked Robert smiling.

'Well, I can't promise that,' she teased.

'Indiana Jones.'

To her horror and embarrassment, a spray of coffee left Rachel's mouth. She grabbed a wad of tissues and apologised profusely.

But Robert was laughing. 'That's quite a reaction!'

When they'd both recovered, he told her he'd always had an interest in archaeology.

'I was a real nerd, I loved ancient history too. Of course, Indiana Jones came after I was at school...' he winked at her. 'But that was never going to pay the bills so...here I am.'

'I wanted to be a hairdresser, I told you about that.' He nodded before she continued, 'I loved seeing how happy customers were when they left the salon, and I couldn't wait to be qualified. But now...I like helping people.'

One coffee turned into two. Along with the sharing of a slice of chocolate cake.

As they parted Robert turned to her and said, 'Rachel, would you like to go out to dinner one night?'

Chapter Twenty-eight

Rachel, Rima, and Lin were crammed into Rachel's bedroom. Rosie was on Lin's phone, watching proceedings via WhatsApp.

'You're all mad!' said Rachel.

Rima and Lin were acting like teenagers. Strewn across Rachel's bed was a selection of outfits.

'I don't know why I can't just wear my black trousers,' she grumbled, only to be shouted down by her friends. Secretly, she was delighted by the attention and fuss.

'Try this one on next,' said Lin.

Rima had taken an old red dress of Rachel's and smartened it up by sewing on a new lace white collar. She also fixed the tear at the bottom of the dress, so it was barely visible.

Rima zipped her up to the cry of oohs and ahs.

Rachel looked in the mirror and had to admit it did suit her.

'That's the one,' said Rosie giving a thumbs up.

'Thank you so much Rima,' Rachel said hugging her friend.

She bent down to get her black court shoes, only to see them snatched out of her hands by Lin.

'What—' exclaimed Rachel.

Lin produced a pair of red shoes, flat with a white bow.

'You're roughly my size, try these,' she said.

Lin was right, they looked perfect with the dress.

Robert was due to pick her up at 7 pm. She tried to put him off, said she could just meet him somewhere. But he had insisted. She was nervous about going out to dinner with him anyway but showing him how she lived only added to her stress levels.

Once she'd shooed her friends out, she made sure she had everything in her bag. She then checked her face in the mirror. Lin wanted to do her make-up, but Rachel had drawn the line at that. She was not going to pretend to be something she wasn't. She was nearly fifty-eight and had a lifetime of wrinkles to show for it. But her hair was freshly washed, her fringe behaving itself for once. She'd been trying to eat better and walking more; she had a healthy glow — enhanced by her red lipstick.

She heard the knock at the door and took a deep breath.

The first thing she saw was not Robert, but a bouquet of gerberas. His face peeked around them smiling. 'Too much?' he said.

She laughed. 'Robert they're lovely, thank you.' She was feeling a little overcome as she couldn't remember the last time anyone had brought her flowers.

Robert admired the vase that Katie had given her. Rachel knew she was talking too fast, her hands sweating as she clumsily put the flowers in the vase. She liked that he didn't try to compliment her on anything about the flat, to make something up. It is what it is, and Rachel was impressed he seemed to sense she wouldn't want him to say something just for the sake of it.

They had driven to a seafood restaurant. The conversation was easy, relaxed as they caught up on what they'd been doing. By the time she was tucking into her fish, her nerves had gone.

Robert was telling her about his three boys.

'Barry lives in London, he's a lawyer. Kieran is in Sydney, he's a social worker, and my youngest Callum is at uni, studying computer science.'

'Gosh,' said Rachel. 'You must be very proud.'

Robert looked serious. 'About their careers? Yes, but I'm prouder of the people they are, they're good men. I think, and my late wife thought the same, jobs are one thing, but it's the person you are that counts.'

Rachel stared at him, it was such a wonderful sentiment, and to hear it voiced made her feel quite emotional.

'What about you, Rachel, did you ever marry?'

He must have seen the look on her face. 'I'm sorry, I didn't mean to pry...I just thought...'

For the first time since she'd known Robert, he looked flustered.

'No, it's fine, honestly. No I never married.'

As much as she was feeling comfortable with Robert, she wasn't ready to tell him about Geoffrey.

She told him about her mother and Rosie.

'I was never...I was very shy; I never knew what to say. And I didn't have brothers or cousins, I just...Rosie was the talkative one, she always knew what to say, and she was funny. I sort of just tagged along.'

'Looking after your mother like that, that must have been hard.'

'I don't want to say I had no choice, because I did, but she brought me up, sacrificed so much for me, I didn't think twice about it,' she blushed as she felt his tender gaze on her.

They talked about their favourite old movies: 'Sound of Music,' said Rachel, 'hands down the best.'

'Rubbish,' scoffed Robert. 'A nun dressed in clothes made from curtains? Casablanca all the way!' They giggled like children.

She told him about some of the nursing home residents.

'Some of them don't get many visitors, they just sit with their memories,' said Rachel. 'I try and find time to sit with them or chat but it's so busy on reception.'

'It's not much of a life, ending up like that,' he agreed.

'That's the thing, these men and women have lived lives, maybe they had children, maybe they did wonderful things in their careers. They all have their own story, and it just feels so sad.'

'I guess the lesson is we have to live life to the fullest while we can,' said Robert. 'Ugh,' he said cringing as he slapped his hand on his forehead, 'I sound like one of those self-help books, forget I said that.'

Rachel laughed as she told him about Rosie's obsession with them and soon they were both chuckling again over their dessert.

As they were leaving and Robert was helping her with her coat, he said, 'I meant to tell you earlier Rachel, you look lovely in your red dress.'

Later that night she sat in bed mulling over the evening. There were so many things to like about Robert. There had been no awkward silences during their dinner. What she couldn't understand was why a man like him could be interested in her? But he seemed genuinely interested when she spoke about the nursing home job, her job as a cleaner, her friends.

She reflected on an earlier conversation from Rosie. 'Rachel, maybe it's finally time to realise you deserve to have a man who likes and respects you for who you are.'

Four days later she and Robert met for a coffee. Afterwards, they went for a walk, enjoying the sunshine. At one point Rachel stopped short, wincing as she rubbed her knee.

'Are you all right?' asked Robert.

'Fine, just happens now and again,' she said.

'How about we treat ourselves to a drink?' Robert said pointing to the local pub.

The next day there was a knock on the door.

Robert was holding a single rose smiling. 'Close your eyes,' he said.

'Why? What's going on?' she said suspiciously as she grinned back at him.

'Come on, close your eyes or you won't get your surprise.'

Rachel felt a package in her hands and quickly ripped off the paper.

'Oh Robert, you sweet man.' She laughed and reached up, her lips finding his as they slowly kissed, a brand-new knee brace in her hands.

Chapter Twenty-nine

Rachel hurried home after her shift at the nursing home. It had been a busy day. They were short staffed in the dining area, so she helped set the tables for lunch, and wheel some of the residents in, chatting to them all the time about this and that. Then just as she was leaving at 2 pm, one of the staff said there was a backlog in the laundry, so she offered to help sort some clean clothes and deliver them to the residents on Level Three. One resident (his room nameplate said Henry) had been sitting alone in his room and something in his face tugged at her.

'Gosh, it's been a busy morning, would you mind if I joined you for a bit and took the weight off my feet?' she asked him as he put his laundry away.

He looked at her surprised but nodded.

On her way home she thought about Henry. Turns out he had been in the army most of his life, and he had been thinking about the men he had served with in Vietnam. Soon the man had been regaling her with stories. He was visibly cheered by the time she left. Rachel felt sorry for the care workers. Many of them told her they wished they had more time to sit and talk with residents but with the endless caring tasks and lack of staff, there just wasn't time.

Rachel practically ran into her unit, aware that the cleaning job she had been booked for started in an hour. She was due to finish at six, and Robert had insisted on picking her up.

Since their first dinner, they'd been seeing each other regularly. Occasionally they went out to dinner, for a walk, a coffee, and once to the movies. She felt very happy and safe with Robert. She enjoyed being in his arms, liked the way he treated her, the way he made her laugh, and how he genuinely seemed interested in what she had to say. She wasn't ready to take the next step with him, but she was content. Happier than she'd ever been.

Her friends were, to her bemusement, continuing to act like teenagers. Why else would Rima always appear just as Robert arrived to pick her up? Even Amira, who stood on the doorstep, her chubby arms folded as she looked him up and down, seemed to be appraising him and deciding whether he was good enough for her Auntie Rachel. Rosie seemed to delight in sending kissing emojis. And Lin of course was the most direct – 'Has he bought you jewellery yet?'

One night she even cooked for him. Robert paid for all their dinners out and she wanted to do something nice for him in return. She'd made a lamb and potato casserole (no mean feat on her old two-burner stove!) and bought some crusty bread to mop up the delicious juices. Afterwards, they watched a movie (Rachel taking care to ensure Robert didn't sit on a broken spring) while eating the ice cream Robert had bought for them.

Robert, aware of Rachel's request to take things slowly, was cautious when he asked her if she'd like to come to Sunday lunch and meet his boys.

'I know you think it's a big step, but it's just lunch,' he said. He took her hands in his. 'They know I've been spending time with you, and it would be lovely for you all to meet.'

'You've told them about me?' said Rachel surprised.

'Of course! Why wouldn't I? You're important to me Rachel.'

Rachel looked at this kind and lovely man who had come into her life and knew it was time to slowly move forward.

She treated herself to a new floral sundress, which would match perfectly with the red shoes Lin had given her. A few weeks ago, she had bought some foundation and a new lipstick and had gone to Just Cuts to get her hair trimmed. Looking in the mirror she didn't think she had ever looked better. As Rima said to her the other night, her face had happiness written all over it.

Robert had come to pick her up, and it was only a ten-minute drive to the large unit he shared with his younger son. Rachel was so nervous she was sure he could hear her heart beating.

'Right, here we are,' he said opening the front door for her.

Fresh white walls. A huge sofa and matching armchairs in soft grey dominated the lounge room, along with a big screen television and a large coffee table stacked neatly with books and magazines. The floors were hardwood, leading into a large open plan kitchen. There were splashes of colour everywhere she looked – a yellow lamp, a green throw, a ruby red ottoman. It was beautiful.

'G'day Rachel.' She turned to see a tall, muscled shape emerging from the kitchen wiping his hands on a tea towel.

'Rachel, this is Callum,' said Robert.

Rachel extended her hand in greeting and smiled at him, or rather looked up and smiled at him. He had to be more than six feet, thought Rachel.

She handed over the bottle of wine she had brought, as the three of them wandered out to the balcony.

A large wooden table was neatly laid with matching light green plates and cutlery. Glasses were stacked ready for use. The barbecue was fired up, and Rachel could see pots of flowering plants dotted around the balcony.

'Can I help? Can I do anything?' Rachel finally found her voice.

'Not at all, you're our guest,' said Robert.

'Nah, it's all pretty much done, thanks for asking,' said Callum.

'Besides, we're forbidden from doing anything with the barbecue until Kieran gets here. That's his domain,' said Robert.

Rachel helped carry out two large salads, a basket of fresh bread rolls. Robert was behind her bringing serviettes, condiments, butter. Callum put down glasses, a wine cooler, a couple of beers. The table was bursting.

'It's a feast,' said Rachel, smiling as Robert squeezed her hand, giving her a soft kiss on the cheek.

'So, Dad tells us you work at a nursing home?' Kieran said turning to Rachel.

Everyone was now tucking into the perfectly cooked steaks. Robert had just poured Rachel a glass of wine and already she felt very welcomed by the family. Kieran and Callum were easy to talk to, and there was a lot of banter between them.

She described how it was only a part-time role and then, hesitating only for a second, told them how she was also a cleaner.

'Good for you,' said Kieran.

They talked a bit more about the nursing home.

'It's sad how many of the residents don't get many visitors. It breaks my heart,' said Rachel.

'Rachel volunteers there as well when she has time, to sit and talk with them,' said Robert.

Callum exchanged a small grin with his brother, amused at their dad talking up his girlfriend!

'We had one person who was moved into the home by her son, initially for respite. She's now there permanently, and the son has visited only once. I know, more than anyone, about family dynamics but it's hard to see the look in her eyes day after day,' said Rachel.

'It's great you do that,' said Kieran.

'Your dad says you're a social worker? asked Rachel.

'Yes, I'm a Drug and Alcohol Case Worker for a charity,' said Kieran.

Rachel tensed thinking of Leah. Robert looked at her anxiously.

'Everything okay?' asked Kieran.

Rachel was silent for a moment. 'I had a dear friend, she...she died from an overdose.' She blew her nose. 'It's a long story, but I can't imagine how hard your job must be sometimes,' she said.

'Leah was homeless, Rachel took her in,' said Robert looking at her.

'Rachel, there's a lot more to you than meets the eye,' said Kieran. 'That's an extremely kind and brave thing to do,' he said. 'Sounds like you would have made a good social worker.'

'And how's Taylor?' asked Robert. 'Taylor's a nurse and was working today,' he added for Rachel's benefit.

'She's good, back on night shift next week which,' he looked at his watch 'reminds me, I probably need to head off. We haven't spent much time together this week,' said Kieran getting up.

'No problem, son,' said Robert. 'Give my love to Taylor.'

'What about dessert, do you want some bro?' Callum was cutting a caramel slice and placing what looked like half the contents of the ice cream container on his plate.

Robert looked at his younger son's plate and deadpanned, 'Will there be enough to go around?'

They all laughed.

Kieran left, surprising Rachel with a hug saying he looked forward to seeing her again.

Rachel and Robert sat down again to have their dessert. Callum stood up, busily texting.

'You off?' asked Robert.

'Yep, gotta go,' said Callum. 'Do you want me to make you coffee before I go?'

Callum made them coffee, hugged Rachel, and was out the door, while Robert yelled after him, 'Have you got your keys?'

They sat back amongst the debris of the lunch enjoying their coffee.

'What a perfect day,' said Robert looking at the sun setting.

'It sure was,' said Rachel leaning into him to cuddle.

Rachel knew that this was an important point in her relationship with Robert. If that was indeed what she wanted — a relationship. And she did. She felt physically ill when she thought back to Geoffrey and remembering how she thought she was in love with him. She now knew it wasn't love.

But she had to be honest with Robert. She was who she was because of what she had been through. Robert knew she had struggled to make ends meet but he didn't know she had been so close to being homeless. He didn't know about Geoffrey, how she had been completely fooled by him; about the miscarriage and what that did to her. He didn't know the depths to which she had sunk when she lost the SalesPlus job, that she had lost Amira in the park, that she had virtually shut down.

It was time to tell him.

Epilogue

'Rachel, where do you want this?'

Rachel turned to see Kieran holding the large tea urn. She told him where to put it and then turned back to the paperwork she was sorting out.

'Whoa, watch it, Jamal,' she said laughing as he ran past her laughing, trying to catch up with his sister. Amira and Jamal had both taken a shine to Callum and followed him everywhere. He would carry Jamal on his shoulders and Amira never left his side. Even now as he finished painting, they were both by his side, handing him paint brushes he didn't need or trying to climb his leg while he stretched his back.

Rachel checked her list of tasks. Ticking off some, circling others. She nibbled on her pen, trying to remember when Helen from the library said she was going to be there.

'Ok love?' she looked up to see Robert by her side. He'd been helping with the last-minute painting and was wearing an old faded long sleeve denim shirt. She reached up and kissed the tip of his nose, wiping off a dot of white paint.

'How did that get there?' she said smiling.

'I'll give you one guess,' said Robert pointing to Amira who was waving a paint brush around.

Rachel laughed, looking around. 'It's taking shape, isn't it?'

Nine months ago, she and Robert had passed a small shopfront on the main street. By the looks of it, it had been vacant for a while. Peeking in, they saw how decrepit it was inside.

Around the same time, Rachel had been reflecting what it had been like when she was looking for work and feeling isolated.

'I wouldn't have survived without people like Rima, Lin and Leah. But there are lots of people who don't have the...' she searched for the right words '...who find themselves alone, particularly older women, and don't know where to turn.'

'Well, we met through one of the community workshops, so there are services and places trying to help,' said Robert.

'Yes, but you have to know where to find them. Not everyone has the internet or a computer — I didn't — and sometimes people don't need anything specific, they just want...contact, a cup of tea and maybe a chat.' Rachel looked thoughtful.

'What are you thinking about?' asked Robert.

Rachel chose her words carefully before she responded.

'Before I met you, my life was defined by two things – what I went through with Geoffrey and being unemployed.'

When she'd finally plucked up the courage to tell him, he had been horrified and upset by what Geoffrey had done to her.

They were on their way to the movies after what had been a long week for both of them.

'I hate the thought of women going through what I have, I'd like to help but...' she shrugged her shoulders.

Before Robert could respond, Rachel took his hand. 'I'm just rambling. Come on, let's get our popcorn.'

But an idea was forming in Rachel's head. A drop-in centre targeted at women but especially older women. She knew from her own experience how easy it was to become isolated, when a friendly face made all the difference. A welcoming place where they could get information on government services or charities but also just a place for a cup of tea or something to eat, a chat with other women who were going through something similar. She thought back to the times when she had to start over, to try to get back on her feet. She would have welcomed such a place.

Why was she even thinking about it, she would chide herself? Life was good. She was enjoying her work. Even better was her relationship with Robert. Since those early days they had gone from strength to strength. After being worried about telling him about her spiralling after losing the SalesPlus job, much to her bemusement, he was decidedly underwhelmed by her confession.

'You drank too much and missed your Outplacement Services meeting, you slept in, and were a little lax with your personal hygiene, is that it?

'Are you joking?' exclaimed Rachel. 'It was bad, and what about how I treated my friends, and almost losing Amira?'

'Are they still your friends?' asked Robert.

'Well, yes...but—'

'But nothing. You made some bad choices, but knowing you as I do now, I bet you've already beat yourself up about it and you need to stop,' said Robert.

'That's what Rosie said.'

'Well, Rosie was right.'

The only sticking point in their relationship — and it wasn't even that — was that Robert wanted to get married.

Rachel loved Robert, she was sure of it, but she refused to give up her independence.

'But you know if we're married, I'm not going to stop you doing anything you want to do?' he'd say whenever the subject came up. 'You do love me?' he'd say looking at her like a needy puppy dog.

She'd give him a hug and say, 'Of course I love you,' and try to explain again. 'You're not like anyone I've ever met, and you know how I feel about you, but it's all been such a struggle and I just want to enjoy what I've achieved,' she paused as she struggled to put into words what she meant. 'All the things that other people took for granted, *I* can now do – a weekly grocery shop, pay my bills on time, get whatever medicine I need, pay for my own movie ticket. I can't tell you what that means to me.'

She would always have to watch what she spent, to budget, there were never going to be luxuries, but she'd never wanted them anyway. God knows when she'd ever be able to give up working but that day seemed a long way off given the enjoyment her new life was giving her.

Surprisingly she found an ally in Kieran for her idea. Perhaps because of the nature of his work as a social worker he understood how she was feeling. It was during one of their many conversations that she floated the idea of the local drop-in centre for older women.

'I know it sounds daft but there's nothing like it in the local area. I looked up some information the other day when I was at the library. Did you know that older women are the fastest growing sector of homeless people in Australia? I think women are somehow less likely to seek out services because of their pride — I know I was — so we have to make it easy for them,' said Rachel.

Kieran had nodded his head, looking thoughtful.

After that everything seemed to move quickly. Kieran had spoken to Rachel and Robert and asked them were they serious about the idea.

'Well yes,' they'd told him.

Kieran told them about Community Service Grants that were aimed at supporting vulnerable groups.

'If we're serious about this, we could put together a plan and apply for a grant,' said Kieran.

'We?' said Robert grinning.

Kieran laughed. 'I have to admit, since Rachel raised it, I've been thinking about it. It is a really good idea and there is a need, and yes, okay Dad, I'd like to be involved,' he said smiling. 'As long as you don't think three's a crowd!'

With Rachel's vision, Kieran's social work experience, and Robert's expertise in writing government documents, they were successful and received a small grant.

Rachel couldn't believe it. Two years ago, she'd been at rock bottom and now look at her life!

They would only be able to open a few days a week and not all day, but it was a start, and they'd have to rely on donations. She was going to continue her job at the nursing home, but scale back on her cleaning shifts.

Everyone was involved. Kieran said she had a knack for convincing people to help.

'You mean nagging?' said Callum one night when he was designing one of the flyers for her on his iPad. She flicked a tea towel at him.

'Right, look at this,' said Callum handing her the iPad.

A community space for older women in crisis
You're not alone.

A smile, a chat, a hot drink, something to eat, support in finding the right services.

That's how we can help you.

Rima was going to provide some light food and act as a translator for any Arabic speaking women. Rachel knew that Rima was going to be invaluable; she had the kindest warmest heart and people naturally gravitated towards her. Helen from the library had donated some books and magazines. Lin was going to volunteer whatever time she could. Rachel reminded her of how much she had been boosted by Lin's gift of a blouse to wear to interviews and the two of them were going to think about how they could help women dress for interviews perhaps through donated clothes? Rosie had sent a donation (which they used to buy a large second-hand table).

Rachel had even contacted Marilyn from the Outplacement Services, who'd offered to run some free sessions for those looking for work. 'How could I resist?' she had said. 'Look at the success you've made of your life, you're a role model!'

Leah's five hundred dollars helped get the centre up and running.

It would be able to refer women to whatever services they might need. Kieran had provided a range of contact information and resources to help women who were looking for work, facing homelessness, fleeing domestic violence, or needing help with mental health or addiction.

He'd also put together some simple clear posters on how to access government services. He'd been interested to hear about Rachel's experience.

'If you don't have the internet, don't have a computer at home, it's hard to know how to access these services. It can be so overwhelming,' she'd told him.

They also made sure everything they had was translated into several languages. Kieran was encouraging her to do a TAFE course on community care, which she was excited about.

And now here they were, ready to open the next day. Rima and Ali had stacked the cups, saucers, plates, and cutlery near the hot water urn and made sure there was enough tea and coffee. Kieran and Taylor had organised all the brochures and posters. Callum and a friend from uni had just finished the painting, the walls now a sparkling white. Amira and Jamal were helping (or hindering) Helen stack books and magazines. Lin was cleaning the table and sorting out the colourful cushions and throw on the sofa. Vanessa and her husband had helped haul away the rubbish. Bev had set up all the social media promoting its opening.

Robert was setting out drinks and chips and made sure everyone had a glass before he cleared his throat and went to stand by Rachel.

Trembling with nervous energy, Rachel looked around at the little group, and then down at the scrap of paper in her hands.

'I'm not going to say much because I'm not one for speeches,' she paused. 'It wasn't that long ago that I needed a place like this. I was one of the lucky ones. I had Rima and Ali and those two,' she said, laughing as she pointed to Amira and Jamal, who looked up guiltily from snatching a chocolate biscuit each. 'People like Lin. They helped me get through it.'

She'd spoken to Rosie earlier. 'Your mum would be so proud,' Rosie said.

'She would, but Rosie, you know I'd never be able to do anything without you pushing and encouraging me,' she'd told her friend.

'Loneliness is difficult. A two or three-minute conversation with Helen when I went to the library meant a lot to me because it was sometimes the only social contact I would have all day. I read the other day that loneliness can be as dangerous to one's health as smoking.

'Bev then gave me a chance. I'm not special, but I feel special because I've made it through. I now want to assist others. And I'm so grateful that you,' she gestured to everyone in front of her, 'feel the same way because this would not be possible without you.' She wiped away a tear.

Robert smiled and nodded at her, giving her the confidence to continue.

'Leah and I would often joke about how different we were. She taught me swear words I'd never even heard of,' she said as everyone laughed.

'We would talk late in the night about anything and everything. We talked about how easy it was for people to fall through the cracks, how everyone needed somebody in their corner.

'That's why this is so important; together we can help people get through the tough times in their life,'

'And so, with that, let's open,' — Callum pulled a sheet away from the wall he had been painting — '*Leah's Corner.*'

-END-

www.ingramcontent.com/pod-product-compliance
Lightning Source LLC
Chambersburg PA
CBHW050354030726
47503CB00006B/1845